"*I WANT YOU*"

she breathed. She snaked her arms around him and closed in. What followed was tempestuous and terribly flattering—until Mark Hood discovered she wanted him dead.

A unique attempt on his life gives Hood his first lead to Dominat. Dominat's domain is a nether-world inside a volcano where electronics have brought the art of torture to exquisite refinement. Dominat has two things Hood must get: a weapon that can destroy the world's defenses, and Tremayne, an Intertrust agent posing as a famous physicist.

But once Hood is inside the citadel he's dead. Unless Murimoto's karate-killer hands can throw a mortal Lucifer from his throne—a throne in the pit of Devil Mountain.

Other SIGNET Thrillers by James Dark

THRONE
OF
SATAN

~~~~~~~~~~~~~~~~~~~~~~~~~

James Dark

A SIGNET BOOK

Published by
THE NEW AMERICAN LIBRARY, Inc.,
in association with Horwitz Publications, Inc.

SIGNET TRADEMARK REG. U.S. PAT. OFF. AND FOREIGN COUNTRIES
REGISTERED TRADEMARK—MARCA REGISTRADA
HECHO EN CHICAGO, U.S.A.

SIGNET BOOKS are published by
The New American Library, Inc.,
1301 Avenue of the Americas, New York, New York 10019

PRINTED IN THE UNITED STATES OF AMERICA

THRONE
OF
SATAN

THE TALL, powerfully built man scraped his chair along the floor as he rose to speak.

"Gentlemen, there will be a change in our plans," he announced.

There were nearly one hundred men in the huge room, sitting around an enormous carved mahogany table. All eyes were turned to the head of the table, watching the speaker.

"We've suffered a temporary setback," he went on, bathing in the respect tinged with fear that was reflected from his listeners' eyes. "Borja bungled the job." He held up his hand, forestalling an unlikely interjection. "Yes, I know, the operation was initially a success, but Borja allowed himself to be hijacked and the core of our nuclear reactor is now back in the hands of the authorities. Borja has been given his instructions. He is to destroy his house on Little Cayman Island, then report directly to me." He shrugged, eloquently spreading his hands. "At least our kidnapping plan is not wasted—we have the scientist, Battersby, who will arrive with Borja. But, gentlemen, we must bring Sugarstrike forward. Our enemies have been warned now, so there is not a moment to lose. The new time will now be tomorrow night— Thursday. Midnight."

The tension lay heavily in the room like a thick fug of cigarette smoke.

The speaker's eyes flicked lightly over the faces beneath him. His thin lips curved in a half-smile.

"The man responsible for the failure of our operation is an American who was acting as bodyguard for Battersby. His name is Mark Hood." He paused and then his lips clamped tightly together. "He got the reactor from us—but he did not get Battersby. And I intend to make sure that Mr. Hood does not trouble us again."

CHAPTER
ONE

~~~~~~~~~~~~~~~~~~~~~~~~~~~~

IT WAS an unreasonable gesture. Perhaps for an Inter-trust agent in such a predicament it could be labeled plain damn stupid. But then it is difficult, even when wrecked on a shallow bank in a gale in the Caribbean Sea, to toss overboard the training of a lifetime. So Tommy Tremayne groped forward in the big stateroom of the grounded *Barracuda* and grabbed by the scruff of his long black hair Senor Pedro Girón y Borja, the Spanish gentleman who had tortured him and come very close to killing him. Tremayne, posing as the brilliant English physicist, Charles Battersby, had been kidnapped by Borja and his thugs. Now the time had come for retribution.

It was night, though starlit. The boat's lighting had failed. The stateroom was dark, and vociferous with the punching of waves against the boat's shivering hull, but the hatchway opening topside showed as a rectangle of fainter gloom. Tremayne dragged his load toward it.

Struck on the forehead by a toppling bookcase as the *Barracuda* had rammed herself on the Serrana Bank, Borja was still unconscious. At this moment, also in the same condition, Mark Hood, Tremayne's fellow Intertrust agent, was being heaved aboard the United States Navy hydrofoil some thirty yards westward along the Bank. But Tremayne could not know that Borja's curare-tipped dart had taken effect on his friend and colleague after Hood had delivered the reactor core to the hydrofoil and started back for Tremayne. Tremayne's present concern was to get out of the boat.

A wind-piled wave rushed at the boat and struck like a steel gauntlet. The vessel shook, and groaned in protest as she was clubbed over farther on her side. How in hell could he drag this dead weight up the ladder? Tremayne wondered. For a second his common sense fought with his character and training and told him to leave the bastard where he was. Training won, however. A United States destroyer had been blown open back there in the Panama Canal, and certain people would be interested in questioning the man responsible. Tremayne gripped his fingers around the collar of Borja's shirt and began to haul.

He almost fainted with the pain spurting from his fingertips. He had Borja to thank for that, for it was Borja who had ordered the bamboo splinters driven in beneath his fingernails. Yet Tremayne slipped his arms beneath Borja's armpits in a hugging hold, hearing even through his pain the ominous grind and groan of the boat's straining timbers. He had managed to reach the foot of the ladder and was staring hopelessly at the tilted barrier when the sea lent a hand.

Like troubles, big waves usually come in threes. The first one came rolling down from the north and its base met the Bank. The wave tripped itself. A tonnage of crest toppled and thundered over the boat in a liquid avalanche of flung white. The stateroom was filled with a cavernous roar. Following closely, the second wave struck and broke the boat's weakened back. She split like a match snapped between fingers, tearing open the stateroom to the sea. Tremayne was hurled backward onto the swilling deck. But he still had his bear hug clamped around Borja when the third wave came smothering in and tossed both of them like flotsam through the gap and into the sea.

Tremayne and his burden were swept along the Bank by the surf. Opened up, held resistant against the Bank, the *Barracuda* was breaking up. It was right then that the captain of the Navy hydrofoil, seeing Borja's boat go, decided to get the hell out of there before his own craft suffered similar treatment. She was designed to skim over water, not bash herself against waves.

Tremayne's head broke surface. The bottom was only about four feet down and his feet thankfully found it. He held Borja's head clear and put his shoulder to the surf, reeling back but not losing his footing as each wave rushed at them. Above the wind's howl he thought he heard a different, shriller voice—this was the hydrofoil's gas turbines as it headed north, skimming over the water toward Jamaica. But with the night and the spray Tremayne could see nothing, and thus failed to recognize that Hood's rescue effort had failed. Yet he did see what was coming for him a few feet away, and recognized harshly what this portended.

Borja was unconscious and helpless, but one of his Jamaican thugs had survived. The man was heading for

Tremayne laboriously now through the broken water. Having no weapon himself, the Intertrust man was relieved, more than fearful, to see that the Jamaican held only what looked in the starlight like a balk of timber.

The Jamaican halted in front of him, shaking his head to clear the water from his eyes. He braced his feet apart and without preliminary lifted the piece of timber and struck.

Tremayne was no karateist as was Mark Hood, but he had won a boxing Blue at Oxford. Still holding Borja, he leaned his upper body swiftly back and sideways. The timber ended its swipe with a solid thump. In the wind Tremayne felt rather than heard this, for the blow landed on Borja's unfeeling shoulder. Then the boxer's fist was moving.

Tremayne aimed for the bared throat and he reached it. The Jamaican dropped his length of timber. His head arched back and his mouth gaped. But he was still on his feet.

Tremayne had had enough. All his restraint had dropped away from him. Anger took its place. Often enough he had watched Hood at karate training, even once in Tokyo acting as his manager. He stiffened his fingers in the *shuto* and with all that was left of his strength he crashed the edge of his palm against the side of the Jamaican's neck.

Even this crudely delivered the *shuto* can be a paralyzing blow. The Jamaican lurched sideways, lost his footing, and went under. His mind coldly deliberate, Tremayne bent down, found the man's neck, clamped his fingers around it, and held the head under.

After a moment the squirming ceased. Tremayne started to count. He had reached ninety, braced there with his arm under the water and Borja humped against his hip, when an alien sound reached him from the sky.

This sound was quite different from the wind's rush and the surge of waves; there was a solid swishing chop to it. Tremayne let go and looked up. Outlined against the stars, its powerful light searching the water, a helicopter lowered closer to the sea.

Kept below during the chase, Tremayne had not seen the helicopter, after having been fired on by Hood from the hydrofoil, recover and deliver the reactor core to Borja on the *Barracuda*. Now his exhausted mind could come up with only one interpretation of a chopper's presence over the Bank—God knew where Mark Hood and the U.S. Navy boat were, but sure enough, here was the rescuing vehicle they must have radioed for. Weakly Tremayne waved his free arm, even though it was obvious he'd been sighted.

And when two men dressed in scuba gear dropped from the helicopter's pontoons he was still unalarmed. They waded up to him, with shoulders pushing into the surf, and the first one took hold of Borja. An arm circled and a yellow belt came snaking down on a thin steel wire.

"Thank God," Tremayne said, too relieved to know or care that his words were whipped away by the wind.

The second diver was level with him. A face peered into his and then Tremayne was forced forward as his hand was thrust up between his shoulder blades and a big arm crooked around his throat.

He tried to speak and could not. And he knew.

As soon as Borja was winched on board, the belt came down again. Tremayne went up, swaying in the wind, trying to block from his mind the thought of what lay ahead of him, telling himself he could not have lasted much longer down there, and gaining no comfort at all from his frying-pan-to-fire jump. They hauled him roughly inside. Here, though clattering with noise, there was, blessedly, no wind. He slumped on the metal deck against the fuselage, watching dully as both divers came inboard, then feeling the aircraft lift away. A weak voice nearby said, "You got him? Good," and Tremayne knew that Borja was both alive and conscious. He felt no uplift of spirit.

Glancing at his adversary, Tremayne saw that his forehead was ridged, and through the black beard his mouth showed as a straight tight line. The Spanish gentleman had lost his suavity. He had also lost the vital box of reactive material from the atomic-powered American destroyer that Borja's plasma beam had sunk in the Panama Canal. The Englishman's mind was still a haze of pain and weariness but quite clearly he recalled Hood taking the box to the hydrofoil. He breathed a silent sigh of relief.

Borja levered himself upright. One of the scuba divers helped him aft to stand above Tremayne where he stood looking down at the Englishman, his eyes steady and cold.

"The lead box," he said. "Who has it?"

Tremayne's smile was as close to a sneer as his bruised face could manage. "You mean you've lost it, Borja? Now you can't continue with your pretty little scheme to immobilize the world's navies, can you?"

Borja kicked him in the ribs. "Who has it?" It was smarter to tell him the truth, now that the box was safe.

Tremayne still smiled as he said, "The U.S. Navy has it, old chap."

"You lie."

Borja lifted his foot, then lowered it. His eyes glowed.

"You can do better than that," Tremayne said. "The Navy really does have your little prize. That big fellow you were about to shoot when we ran aground took it with him."

Borja said viciously, "He did not bother to take you."

Tremayne had insisted on the box going first. He kept his face masked. "Naturally, the box would come first."

The scuba diver leaned sideways and whispered in Borja's ear. Borja frowned, then looked down at Tremayne.

"My man says you were holding me up in the water."

Tremayne nodded. "Yes. I should have let you drown like a bloody rat."

"You may regret that you did not."

Tremayne was near exhaustion. The ache in his fingers and body was a massive, shooting pain. He still smiled. "No doubt you're right, my friend, but the authorities are on to you. How far d'you think you can get in this thing?"

The Englishman's studied insolence had a restraining effect on Borja. He matched the other's twisted smile.

"I can get to my house on Little Cayman Island. In this weather I can get there before that Navy boat can reach Kingston. We are heading for Little Cayman now at maximum speed. Once there I can make other arrangements to continue my work on a bigger scale."

"You're forgetting something. Radio."

"In this case," Borja said softly, "why should they radio? My boat was wrecked; there could be no survivors. Besides, they have the reactive material so why should they trouble to ask a boat to go to Little Cayman tonight? It would be risky to put to sea in this storm and there is no landing strip on the island. Nothing but a helicopter could get the police there before me. Would they send one in a gale, when I am believed to be dead?"

Tremayne's hopelessness showed and Borja's smile widened into a slit of satisfaction.

"It would seem you will be with us until my experiments are completed, Battersby. If that *is* your name?" he ended quickly.

Tremayne frowned. He had come very close to forgetting his cover. "What d'you mean?" Then he closed his eyes and shook his head tiredly. "Leave me alone, for God's sake."

Borja didn't move. "I'm wondering how a physicist in Jamaica for a technical conference could have managed to call on the Navy so opportunely."

Tremayne realized he had to be careful. Very careful. He sighed. "I imagine our friend the police inspector would know more about that. You blundered, Borja. You were about as artless as a chorus line of elephants doing *Swan Lake*. Now please let me sleep."

Borja looked down at his prisoner. There was a speculative gleam in his eyes. Then he crossed to a small cabinet on the fuselage and came back with a bottle. Into his hand he shook one pill.

"Swallow this."

"Cyanide, or strychnine?"

"The ocean would be more convenient. No, my friend, I want you alive and well to help my future plans. This will kill the pain. Take it."

Tremayne obeyed him, knowing without comfort that Borja spoke truthfully. In less than a minute his lacerated nerves had dulled their shrieking protest, and slumping on the hard deck he slept.

The gale was easing but the helicopter still bucked a strong headwind. Tremayne was allowed almost three hours' rest before a hand shook him roughly awake. In those three hours, his body, wiry and muscular, had retrieved many of its losses, and he awoke comparatively refreshed and alert to find, with a vast and private relief, that the pain had eased to a bearable aching.

"Out," ordered his waker.

Tremayne pulled himself to his feet and limped to the door where he saw in the lightening gray of dawn that the helicopter had come to rest beside the landing of Borja's pier. He stepped ashore. There was the plantation-style house on top of the cliff and nearby the funicular with its electric carriage to lift them upward. Borja was speaking to his waiting men:

". . . thermite flare, and gasoline to make sure. The seaplane is to be ready for takeoff in one hour, with the spare tanks filled to capacity."

"Yes, Don Pedro."

"You," Borja said to Tremayne, "come with me."

At the funicular he halted. He said nothing, just looked at Tremayne and patted the bulge in the pocket of his damp jacket. Tremayne nodded briefly; he was in no position to make any bid for escape. They rode up the funicular in silence and stepped into the big house the Englishman remembered only too well; the house in which he had been kept prisoner and tortured.

"In here."

It was the main bedroom. At Borja's summons, a Jamaican appeared to guard Tremayne, while Borja packed clothes and papers. Tremayne noticed a flickering glow through the windows. Fire. So that was their game, he thought. They were burning all trace of evidence. He realized the extent of Borja's intention when the Spaniard gestured him out into the hall and he saw two Jamaicans busily spraying gasoline from jerry cans. In the bay, the helicopter was a sheet of flame.

"Here," Borja ordered.

Tremayne went in first and the memories flooded back. It was from here that he had broadcast the warning which had taken Hood out in the hydrofoil, and which had brought the big fellow so very close to saving him.

Abruptly, the thought slammed in. They must have seen the boat break up. Hood would believe him dead. And Borja, and all his crew. The file would be closed. No further search, no rescue. God, he must be in shocking shape not to have thought of this before!

The realization bemused him, so that Borja had picked up the radiotelephone and was speaking into it before Tremayne could understand that maybe here was vital information. He forced himself to listen. Borja was speaking Spanish. It was no use. Tremayne didn't speak Spanish. He didn't understand a word. He slumped into a chair. Since Borja had caught him he had endured a harsh ordeal, and right now, for the first time in his career, he was quite without hope.

CHAPTER

TWO

~~~~~~~~~~~~~~~~~~~~~~~~

IT WAS NOT much after dawn when Inspector Owen of the Jamaican constabulary took up his telephone.

All night he'd stayed in the police station, working on Mark Hood's report. This was a masterpiece of brevity, and there was much the inspector did not understand, for the simple reason that the Intertrust agent had left much out. The inspector knew nothing whatever of the Intertrust organization but he did know that Hood was not the rich international playboy type he pretended to be. Owen, a simple man with more than simple tastes, somehow felt as if he were floundering beyond his depth. International intrigue, all that sort of thing; it was much safer just reading about it.

Now, with the phone, he took up a pack of cigarettes. His burned tongue was sore. He grimaced, dropped the pack, and dialed instead.

In distant obedience, a telephone shrilled in the bedroom of a villa out along the Windward Road. It was a pretty villa, fronting a wide lawn which sloped toward a secluded beach. It was owned by Borja, whose agent had rented it to Hood and Tremayne when they first arrived in Jamaica.

The man lying on the bed was awake, and his drawn face looked as if he hadn't slept. His thoughts had been deeply introspective, so that the abrupt shrill of the phone startled him. His hand reached out, revealing an unusual callus along the lower edge of the palm.

"Yes?"

"Mark? This is Dick Owen." This inspector's tone was easy.

"Yes, what is it?"

"I'm flying over to check the house on Little Cayman. Why don't you come along? Now that Borja's dead there's some mopping up to be done."

Hood sat up, and wedging the receiver between his jaw and hunched shoulder, fished for a cigarette from the bedside table. He lit it. "Dick, I know how important it is that we catch Borja, but right now I'm more interested in that boat wrecked on the Serrana Bank."

"The Navy will be looking after that. Borja's my main worry at the moment, or what's left of his organization."

"Okay," he said. "I'll come, but I want to have a look at that boat while it's still there and before the Navy boys clamp it down on the secret list. Besides that, there's

Tremayne. I'd like to bring his body back if possible.
When do we leave?"

"Soon as you're ready. I'll send a car."

"Right, Dick. See you in a few minutes."

From a concrete pad back of the station the police
helicopter rose into a pearly pink sky, heading northwest. Before they were clear of the island, the sun lifted
an orange eyebrow behind them, and then the sea became a blue face winking up at them with a million
bright eyes.

Hood stared down at the sea; he had been a sailor.
The water cast a reflective impact on his eyes, but none
at all in his consciousness. That was too full of other,
bitter thoughts. The pilot was alert enough, but none of
the three men looked up into the high sky.

Which was a pity. The seaplane coming from the direction of Little Cayman Island, even though it was
heading due south away from Jamaica, might have
sparked suspicious interest, and probably interception.
But they were not looking for a seaplane. They knew
Borja had owned the big *Barracuda* and a helicopter; no
one thought of a plane.

The seaplane was looking for everything. Besides Tremayne and Borja, it carried the three men of the helicopter's crew. Every eye was searching both sea and sky,
even Tremayne's. Especially Tremayne's.

Borja had ordered maximum height. But even from so
high the police helicopter, dark against the bright blue
and chasing its shadow, showed plainly. The pilot turned
in his seat and gestured downward. In a moment Borja
raised a hand in acknowledgment of his own sighting.

Tremayne was seated beside him. Physically, at least,
he was feeling much better. Among certain other less
commendable attributes Borja had had a surgeon's training, and had treated Tremayne's damaged fingertips. "I
don't want you dying from septicemia," he had explained
matter-of-factly. Whatever his reason, the treatment had
helped considerably. When he saw the aircraft beneath

them, Tremayne's heart plummeted. The helicopter was far below them, and maintaining a steady heading to the northwest, in an almost opposite direction to their own.

"That is almost certainly a police machine," Borja said.

"Yes."

"You seem less than happy, my friend." Borja chuckled. "You know where it's heading?"

"Yes. I wish them luck."

"They'd need more than luck," Borja said with a smile, "to find anything of value to them at Little Cayman. Still, I suppose the inspector has to test all his theories. Something like a scientist, eh, Battersby?"

Tremayne was beginning to doubt the value of maintaining this facade of the eminent physicist. Sooner or later Borja would tumble to his scientific ignorance. The Battersby cover was beginning to fray about the edges. Though when Borja discovered he wasn't the scientist Battersby, but an impostor, he was as good as dead. Tremayne said:

"All right, you're safe. So where's the risk in telling me where we're going?"

"None at all. We are going to meet my . . . er . . . partner."

Tremayne managed to keep the interest from his eyes. Borja had mentioned his plan to continue development of the lethal plasma beam but had said nothing about a partner.

"Surely there can't be another guy like you?"

But Borja, airborne and with the helicopter a dwindling dot astern, had fully regained his cool suavity.

"You will find him interesting. In fact, he's a scientific genius who is anxious to meet you. But Dominat has a taste for the macabre. You should watch your tongue, if you wish to keep it."

"And where does this other perverted scientist live?"

"On the island of Dominica." Borja's mouth twisted a little and Tremayne thought his eyes narrowed.

Partners, Tremayne decided, carefully noting the sudden change of expression on Borja's face, but maybe not pals. It was only the tiniest crack but there could be no harm in trying to widen it. He filed the impression away in the back of his mind.

Borja went on: "Dominat is the most brilliant mechanical scientist I have ever met. And very shortly we will both be recognized as a potent force throughout the world. When fully developed, my weapon will supplement his inventions to baffle the world powers. You see, Mr. Battersby, we do have a plan—a foolproof plan." He gave a short rasping laugh. "And you, Mr. Battersby, are going to help us."

The police helicopter flew in over the pier at Little Cayman Island, but the fuel-driven heat had reduced Borja's helicopter to a twisted metallic skeleton lying on the bottom; it lay ten fathoms down, and no one spotted the evidence he had been so careful to hide. In any case, all eyes were on the house, or what was left of it.

"Ashes," the inspector grunted. "Still smoking. It'll be too damned hot to search."

Hood's mind was on another tack. For the first time since the Navy hydrofoil had intercepted the *Barracuda* the night before, his face showed some animation.

"That fire's no accident. Who did it?"

"Borja would have left his instructions," Owen said. "No doubt he was prepared for any eventuality. . . . Well, it looks as if all our birds have flown."

Hood shrugged. "You're probably right."

All the same, he was not entirely convinced. There was something nagging him, an abstract tugging-at-his-sleeve. He looked down at the smoking ruin beneath them, then up at Owen.

"Dick, I've got to see that boat. The *Barracuda*."

Owen pursed his lips. "It'll be difficult, Mark. Just before we left I received a call from the Navy. It's out of my hands now."

"Let's get back to the base then, shall we?" Hood suggested. He wanted to see Bill Brennan, the commander of the Navy hydrofoil and a wartime buddy of Hood's. He glanced at his watch. It would take them an hour or so to get back to Kingston. Bill would probably be still in bed.

Bill wasn't. He was down at the waterfront, at the guarded pier where his baby, a flat circular vessel with a rounded bow, was moored.

Bill's hydrofoil was only a prototype and, as he had explained to Hood at their first meeting, would be designed on a large enough scale to carry aircraft and batteries of ICBM missiles. It was fast. The gas and turbine engines would take the craft from New York to Southampton in less than thirty-six hours, the Navy commander had proudly added.

"Hello, Mark." Brennan looked tired. There were dark patches beneath his red-rimmed eyes. He was sitting at his desk, thumbing through a sheaf of message flimsies. "You look beat, too," he said, waving Hood to a chair beside his desk. "Get you some coffee?"

Hood, ignoring the chair, eased his weight onto a corner of the desk. He shook his head. "No, no coffee. Listen, Bill, I want you to do me a favor."

Brennan lit a cigarette, then leaned back in his chair. "What is it now?"

"I want you to take me out to the Serrana Bank."

"In this craft, you mean?" Brennan thoughtfully stroked his jaw, his hand scraping against the light stubble. Then he lay the palm of his hand flat down on top of the pile of papers. "No, Mark. I can't do it."

"Look, it's very important. I've got to see that boat."

"Mark," Brennan began, speaking slowly and distinctly as if he were explaining something to a child, "I stuck my neck out far enough chasing that damn boat before it sank. Luckily, that paid off and we saved the reactor. But now I've made my report. I've been instructed to stand by to take a party of security brass to inspect the wreckage at eleven hundred hours. I'm sorry, Mark, but I . . ."

Hood pushed himself away from the table, towering

over the naval commander. "Hell, what's happened to you, Bill? You getting soft, frightened to take risks anymore? I only want to look at the wreck. We'll be there and back well before your big brass shows up here."

Brennan swiveled his chair away from Hood. "How in blazes did I get tangled in this thing anyway?" he said with a sigh. "I know how you feel, losing your friend and all, Mark, but there's nothing you can do."

"So you were told to stand by at eleven hundred hours," Hood persisted stubbornly. "Your orders say anything about not taking a practice run at dawn?"

Brennan stood up and grinned. "I guess it can't hurt. A practice run, as you say."

It was Hood's turn to grin. He lightly punched his friend's arm. "Come on. We're wasting time."

CHAPTER

THREE

~~~~~~~~~~~~~~~~~~~~~

As THEY SKIMMED over the sparkling water toward the
Serrana Bank, Hood thought about Tremayne. He
winced as the memory of the events of the night before
came back to him; the lance of flame that had shot the
bullet into his still throbbing arm, and Tremayne, hands

bloodied, body bruised purple, smiling through the beaten muscles of his face.

Hood grabbed the pack of cigarettes from the shelf in front of him and lit one, drawing on it so that his cheeks pinched in

And after a minute or so he could think again of his friend, the lanky and laconic Tremayne with the cultured drawl, all steel underneath and always there when the chips were down. It had to come sooner or later; you knew that in this game. But the only close friend he had? How in God's name could you make friends in a job like this? As an Intertrust agent you had no roots; a phone call could send you halfway around the world; there was no chance of establishing normal lasting relationships. You mixed with scum. Then you found someone, a man you trusted more surely than yourself, and the filth took him.

Above the roar of the engines, Brennan, at the controls, pointed ahead. Hood could just make out the patch of dark water that reflected the nearest bastion of the Serrana Bank.

Borja's boat, the *Barracuda,* Hood saw with dismay, had slipped off the edge of the Bank under the constant battering of the waves that had attacked it the night before. Brennan brought the hydrofoil around the edge of the Bank while Hood peered over the edge, trying to sight the dislodged craft.

At last he saw it. He signaled to Bill, who swung the vessel in closer, where it hovered over the spot Hood had indicated. Beneath him, the clear turquoise water splintered into myriad sparkling wavelets.

"I'm going down," Hood called.

Brennan frowned and glanced at his watch. Then he reached down and slid open the door of a cabinet by his knees. From it, he hauled out a neoprene jacket, flippers, an aqualung, and a mask. Hood stripped and hurriedly put on the equipment.

It was cool in the water. Favoring his wounded right

arm, Hood swam slowly, pushing down toward the wreck of the *Barracuda*.

The nose of the boat was caught tight in a crevasse of rock and its hull was rolling precariously on the edge of a narrow shelf. Looking down past it, Hood could only just make out the sandy bottom and, some distance away, what looked like a dark beetle-shaped rock. He swam carefully around the teetering wreck.

It could fall at any moment and if Hood happened to be inside it when it went, it could make a dandy tomb for him. But he had to look inside. There was something he had to know. While he and Dick Owen had been flying over Borja's former stronghold on Little Cayman Island he had begun to wonder. What if Borja weren't dead after all? If he had somehow been rescued, there was the possibility too that Tommy Tremayne was still alive. Since Borja believed the Englishman to be the eminent scientist, Charles Battersby, he'd still think Tremayne invaluable to him in his evil scheme.

Hood swam closer to the boat. The door to the cabin was hanging loosely on its hinges. As Hood propelled himself through, his shoulder brushed against the doorjamb. The boat lurched drunkenly across to one side, then settled. Hood, bracing his feet apart, found his balance. It had been close.

There was no sign of Tremayne's body in any of the cabins, but that wasn't conclusive, Hood told himself. He could quite easily have been washed away. Nor was there any sign of Borja. . . . The little glimmer of hope that had been sparked earlier that morning flared up into a steady flame. There was hope after all. Very carefully, so as not to upset the balance of the boat, he began pulling out drawers and opening cabinet doors.

There were the usual instruments to be found in a boat of this size. There were maps and charts, now soggy and practically undecipherable. Still, Hood decided, they might be useful. He placed them to one side, wedging them into one of the drawers to keep them from floating away.

In another drawer he encountered some resistance. Something was blocking it. He increased his pressure but it still refused to budge. He didn't want to pull too hard in case the sudden jarring movement when the drawer released its hold should be more than the boat could stand. Working his hands inside the drawer, Hood reached for the obstruction with outstretched fingers. He pulled it out carefully.

It was a thin folder fashioned out of soft brown leather with an overhanging flap that was secured with a zipper. On the flap was engraved the single gold initial, *B*.

Picking up the charts from the drawer he pressed them against the brown folder, then, folding the leather container over them twice so that it made a compact little package, squeezed it into his belt. After one last look around he was ready to go. He edged his way out of the cabin, this time without bumping anything. Once, aft, there was a loud crack and groaning from the warping timbers. Hood swam out over the sloping deck, then, at last, he was free. He didn't see anything, certainly noticed nothing out of the ordinary, although he hadn't realized that the beetle-shaped rock he had seen earlier was so close. It was almost directly beneath him now, a few feet from the side of the coral bank. It looked larger, almost like a small whale. Hood turned away. Above, Bill Brennan was waiting for him in the hydrofoil. As Hood began to surface, the monogrammed leather folder and the maps tucked securely in his belt, he didn't suspect any danger.

It came. He didn't know what had warned him. It was a premonition, a defensive mechanism that he had developed through all the years of living with danger, when the sharpness of his reflexes, a split second's timing, was the only boundary drawn between life and death.

Abruptly Hood jackknifed his legs and rolled forward, the fierce kick of his flippers plummeting his body downward. He swung his head as he dived and saw the rushing glint of steel as the spear lanced above his back and then, ten yards away, he saw the man who had fired it.

He had a CO_2 speargun, an elephant gun capable of skewering Hood clean through, and its owner was fast at work reloading. Hood twisted, legs scissoring and big hands clawing at the water as he lunged for his attacker.

With about ten feet still to go he knew he was too late. In water sound travels four times faster than through air. He heard the concussion and saw the bursting discharge of the gas. So close, there was no time to get sideways or down. Automatically, futilely, Hood tensed his abdominal muscles. His whole body crawled as he waited for the tearing entry of the barbed head.

A shafting flash caught his eye to the left. The spear went wide by a yard. It wasn't the aim; it couldn't be. The very power of the gas-propelled gun had saved him. The spear must have been slightly bent. Shot at such tremendous speed it had been deflected by the water's resistance. Hood wasn't concerned with reasons. He put his head down and in he went.

The gun's heavy butt came like a javelin for the glass of his mask. Hood ducked his head. The butt scraped between his shoulder blades. His fingers gripped the other's wrist. The gun dropped. It zigzagged down, unseen. For a second both bodies hung there, hands joined, free hands paddling for stability, while each man stared through the glass of the other's mask. Hood saw a wide brown face and eyes that were almost black, and knew his enemy was Jamaican. And strong.

The man's left hand went to his lead belt, to the sheath clipped there. It came up and the filtered light gleamed evilly on the knife's stainless steel. The blade lunged for Hood's belly.

Quite automatically, thirty feet below the surface of the Caribbean Sea, Hood slipped into karate. Here through the water's resistance he could not effectively use a *shuto* chop, but he did not need a forceful blow, only deflection and then contact. As the knife arm straightened on the lunge Hood released his grip. He used both hands in the *soto uke,* drawing swiftly a semicircle that knocked the arm aside and then, as his body twisted, he gripped the wrist with his left hand and jabbed his right elbow hard into the Jamaican's rib cage. And now the knife arm was over Hood's left shoulder, twisted so that the inside of the elbow faced upward, and both his hands were gripped around the wrist. Fierce and sharp, Hood jerked down.

For a second, on the fulcrum of Hood's shoulder blade, the Jamaican was lifted upward behind him. But he weighed two hundred pounds, and his lead-weighted belt pulled back against the water's buoyancy. He could lift no farther, yet the dreadful pressure was still hauling down on the lever of his arm. With a small snap the bone broke. The arm dangled. The knife dropped.

Gun and knife. Hood's own arm wound was throbbing and he felt tired but he knew he had his man. They had moved around behind a narrow promontory that jutted out from the bank, and glancing up, he saw that the hydrofoil was out of sight. He could see white splinters of bone sticking out through the man's brown skin. Hood flippered clear.

Then he turned, and knew it was not all over yet. The native had guts, Hood conceded. He was also still armed. His good hand was at his side, tugging. It came up gripping a short hand spear. Hood cursed his carelessness. While still close in there he should have ripped off the mask. Now he had a barbed head to face, with a good strong arm behind it.

His eyes squinted, trying to see more clearly. No doubt about it. There was no barbed head at all, just a blunt-ended stick.

The Jamaican came toward him. The thing he carried was thrust out in front. Light glinted dully on something yellow, like brass. It was brass. A cold twist of fear clutched Hood's guts. That shining blunt end was a 12-gauge shotgun cartridge screwed onto the head of the spear. It was used to kill shark and grouper. It would need only a jab against his back or belly, or any solid part of his body, to explode.

The Jamaican was only feet away when Hood made his decision. No man could stay under much longer with the head of that broken radius sticking through the skin. Hood jerked his body away and swam downward.

He was up against a zombie of a man. A glance over his shoulder told him this. Obviously the Jamaican was an expert scuba diver, but there was that peculiar purposefulness that in many cases was prompted by fear. He was still coming, that ugly spear held extended ahead of him, and something had to be done about it. The man was now between him and the hydrofoil.

Hood landed on the sandy bottom and turned. The Jamaican settled a few yards away.

The bottom gave the wounded hunter some advantage over swimming, but not as much as it did to Hood's karate-trained feet. Obeying the basic tenet of his weaponless art, he did not move forward offensively, but waited.

Crouched forward to lessen resistance, the Jamaican came toward him. Hood saw the dark stain drifting from his dangling arm but he forced the thought of sharks from his mind, to keep it receptive. Normally he looked in an opponent's eyes, for from there intention was most often telegraphed, but this was impossible at any distance from the mask. Hood kept his sight on the spear arm, coldly aware that a solid touch anywhere would produce a wound much more crippling than the one he had given his enemy. Taut-minded but with muscles relaxed, he waited.

The spear jabbed. Hood's trained instincts told him it was a feint. It was. Then almost immediately the arm was fully extended and the lethal cartridge lanced for Hood's midriff. This time he moved.

Feet solidly planted, he was in the wide-apart *shiko dachi* stance, which allowed his upper body to move swiftly to the left. There was an instant of reactive fear as he felt the spear graze his side, but the touch was glancing. Then Hood was forward and under the arm, gripping and reversing it, and now he was behind the Jamaican, forcing the spear hand high between the shoulder blades. The hand's grip relaxed and Hood slid the spear clear. His mind blocked coldly to pity, filled solely with intention, he leaned against the protection of his hunter's back, swept his hand around sideways, and jabbed the spear against his opponent's belly.

A movable firing pin struck the primer. The cartridge exploded with a water-damped crack. The charge of shot blasted forward and in. The Jamaican was a big man but his body was thrust back. Then it sagged down and lay curled on the bottom, where a darkness began to crawl over the white sand.

Hood went as fast as he could, slanting upward for the surface. As he came around the promontory to where the *Barracuda* was still perched on the ledge and saw, thankfully, the bulky reflection of the hull of Bill Brennan's hydrofoil, he saw something else. It was just below him, on the seabed. For a moment he tried to place what it was. It was beetle-shaped and looked vaguely familiar. Then he remembered. He had seen it before and had thought it was a rock. It wasn't a rock. It was moving, running along the seabed, negotiating the uneven surfaces in much the same manner as a tank. It *was* some sort of a tank, Hood realized with a start. It was moving away from him, disappearing into the murkiness of the depths.

Hood kicked himself violently to the surface. He ripped the mask away from his face and shouted to a surprised Brennan, who came quickly to the side to help him aboard.

"Sub. There's a sub down there." He swung his legs over the side and stood on the deck, the water dripping from his lithe, athletic body to form a spreading pool on the planking at his feet.

Brennan started to say something, but before he could speak there was an explosion. It came from beneath them—from, Hood guessed, about the position where the *Barracuda* had been—and, as the shock waves hit the hydrofoil and a massive bubbling of boiling froth surged up from beneath the water, catching the vessel on one side and whirling it around like a spinning top so that the two men lost their balance and sprawled across the bucking deck, Hood knew what had happened. He knew very well what had happened. Borja's men had returned to destroy the *Barracuda* and any evidence that might give the investigating authorities a clue to either the Spaniard's whereabouts or the scope of his operations.

They had detailed a man to intercept and kill Hood; then, assuming that had been done, had gone ahead and laid the explosive charges in the *Barracuda's* hull.

Hood waited for another explosion. There was none. One must have been sufficient. He scrambled to his feet.

"For Christ's sake," Brennan bellowed. "What happened?" Then as a cold thought seemed to strike him, he wheeled on Hood. "My God, Mark, you didn't . . . ?"

Hood shook his head. "Of course not. There was someone else down there, and a sub. More like a tank, really. It was running along the seabed on tracks."

He explained what had happened while he had been in the water. Brennan heard him out, but there was still a doubtful expression on his face when Hood finished telling his story.

All around them the sea was littered with jagged slivers of timber.

"There's going to be hell to pay when the security boys find out what's happened." Brennan sighed. "Did you find what you were looking for?"

"I don't know," Hood replied thoughtfully. "I didn't find Tommy, if that's what you mean. Nor did I find friend Borja."

On the way back to Kingston, changed into his dry clothes, Hood opened the brown leather folder he had found stuck in the cabin drawer. Inside was another, smaller plastic folder which contained a single sheet of thin rice paper. He held it up to the light. There was something typewritten on it.

It was headed by the word SUGARSTRIKE; then, beneath that, one line: I ROSE AND ON THE THRONE OF SATAN SATE—5 3. That was all.

Hood frowned at the paper for a few moments, then placed it on the desk beside him.

The charts weren't able to tell him much. They were Admiralty charts of the Caribbean area, and as far as he could see, there were no endorsements on them. Still, when they were properly dried out and he had the necessary aids to go over them carefully, there just might be some clue that would lead him to Borja, or his associates.

The sheet of paper he had taken from the folder was one clue. He was sure of it. It meant something—something important—for Borja to have taken the trouble to keep it snug and secure in a waterproof covering. Hood picked up the sheet and carried it across to Brennan.

"What do you make of it, Bill? Mean anything to you?"

Brennan looked at it, then shook his head. "No, it doesn't."

"There's something about that phrase that rings a bell," Hood said. "I wish I knew why."

Brennan looked across at the charts. "Are you going to hold onto those?"

"Yes. Maybe they'll be able to tell me something."

"I still don't like it."

"You don't have to know anything about it. As far as you're concerned you don't know anything. You can still take your security wallahs out to the Bank and look just as surprised as they do when they find out what's happened to the *Barracuda*—if there's any trace of it left."

For the remainder of the journey back to port Hood kept studying the sheet of rice paper. If only he could remember.

And there was something else. There seemed to be something wrong with the sentence—a word out of place, or misspelled.

"The number—fifty-three—that could be your code reference," Brennan suggested.

Hood lit a cigarette. "Could be," he murmured. "It's obviously some sort of a message—a summons perhaps? Now, why would Borja take so much trouble to preserve this sheet of paper? Maybe he's not number one in the organization after all. Fifty-three. Could mean anything." He drew deeply on his cigarette, pulling the smoke back into his lungs, then he sat up with a start.

"Bill, say he'd been summoned to a meeting or whatever, he would have to be informed of the time of the meeting. The date. What's the date today?"

"May second."

"Fifty-three. Five-three. Third of May. Tomorrow."

"So maybe you've got a date," Brennan said. "What about the rest of it?"

"It's a start. The location of that meeting might be hidden in this sentence somewhere."

"You don't have much time," Brennan observed.

Hood realized that. It mightn't be a meeting, but he had a feeling that something was going to occur tomorrow, something in which Borja had had a hand, which meant that, whatever it was, it wouldn't be very pleasant. Very carefully, he placed the sheet of paper back in its folder.

If this was as big as it was beginning to shape up, he would need some help. He decided that, as soon as he got back to Kingston, he was going to put a top priority call through to his headquarters in Geneva.

He was almost certain now that they had only scratched the surface of the truth. Already Borja had demonstrated his fantastic underwater plasma ray; they knew its extraordinary power to alter ships' compasses and to fire missiles from destroyers.

If Borja were still alive he'd certainly be complying with plans to put that power to further use.

CHAPTER

FOUR

DOMINICA, BORJA HAD told him cosily, with Puerto Rico and Cuba invisibly far to their left, was the most savage, the most mysterious, and the least developed island in the West Indies. The Spaniard was affable because his destination was close; he knew he was not being followed.

Tremayne was feeling stiff, and his fingers still ached. Not very long ago he had come close to rescue, and the same common sense that warned him not to be hopeful also had him trying to pump Borja in case there was another opportunity. He did this with characteristic deviousness.

"Come on, Borja," he said, "You can tell me what your game is now. I'm hardly likely to escape, am I?"

"You are right. My dear sir, I came very close to admiring your coolness. A British trait I have felt to be rather schoolboyish and futile. Still, I can't help but admire you. As to our plans, I'm afraid you will have to wait until you have met my partner. You will like him, I'm sure. He is most fluent."

There was a brief silence, then Borja pointed ahead. "Ah, there is our destination."

For some minutes land had been in sight—set greenly in blue, an island shaped like a fat grub and running from north to south.

"On the northern tip," Borja explained, "you can see rather a large upthrust of volcanic rock. It is called Morne au Diable." He smiled. "Unless you are cooperative, you may find that Devil Mountain is aptly named."

Something ghostly feathered up Tremayne's spine but he otherwise ignored the threat. "Your partner lives on the slope of a volcano?"

"No, my friend; inside."

Tremayne looked up inquiringly but Borja did not elaborate.

The plane was banking over the northern tip of the island, heading for a fairly large bay indenting the coastline just below where it turned to run southward. Because he was still alive, and a trained observer, Tremayne concentrated again on seeing all he could, although the odds against his putting it to use were overwhelming.

The coastline was mostly precipitous and heavily indented with bays and coves. Below him lay the dense greenery of majestic sandbox and mahogany trees, with here and there the green-and-white-leaved splash of a great cannonball tree, a primeval forest reaching to and surrounding the bare crusty cone of the Morne au Diable. Its ulcered mouth reached up like a white rock from a green sea.

The plane sideslipped in over the rocky shoulder of the bay. Tremayne had time to see a large village, then they were rising up the side of the mountain toward the peak.

"That village is also part of what I might call our little empire," Borja explained. "It is called, simply, Dominat."

"The name of your partner?"

"That's right." Borja settled back in his seat and locked his fingers across his stomach. "Now you will see something quite unique."

Tremayne turned away from Borja and stared out the window. He had seen something on Borja's face—something that secretly pleased him. The Spaniard was scared. Although he was smiling, the smile never reached his eyes.

As the plane banked away from the top of the mountain and beamed in again in a wide circle, the Englishman looked down into the dead crater beneath them. A wide steel platform ran across its diameter. The plane was dropping. It passed right over the top of the mountain, then turned again, bearing down on the ribbon of glittering gray metal. They were about to land right there on the mountain, Tremayne realized.

Now that they were practically level with the runway, it looked much longer. The plane was small and maneuverable.

There was a squeal as the wheels gripped the rough steel. Then the aircraft was turning. They stopped and the silence, after the steady hum of the motors, was almost tangible.

"The end of the ride?" Tremayne asked.

"We will wait here," Borja said. He was not smiling now.

They waited. Then, beneath them, was a distant hum of machinery, and without being aware of any movement, Tremayne saw that the inner walls of the crater seemed to be closing in over them. Then he realized that they were being carried down, plane and all, on top of the platform into the bowels of the mountain.

Tremayne wondered what sort of a man could have organized all this.

"My partner is most resourceful." Borja was giving out with the propaganda talk again. Tremayne wondered if he were trying to boost his own confidence. "That platform wasn't designed only for planes. Most of the traffic that comes here, from the mainland and other islands, are helicopters, of course."

They were still descending. It was getting dark. Tremayne guessed that they must be nearing the bottom. Soon it was so dark that he was unable to see through the windows.

Then they stopped. There was a heavy clank of metal. Tremayne saw that they were still moving, only now they were being drawn sideways into the thick side wall of the mountain.

A bright blaze of light hammered into his eyes. He blinked until his eyes became accustomed to the glare.

"Come on," Borja urged, pulling himself to his feet. He began to walk toward the door of the plane which had already been opened. A short metal ladder had been hooked to the side for them to climb down. They were in an enormous chamber which had been carved out of the rock. The sides and the roof were smooth. Tremayne looked around him in amazement.

Against the far wall of the cavern, so far away that they looked like toys, stood a row of helicopters. Tremayne looked back at the plane. Already a mobile generating unit had been brought up to it and a team of mechanics in spotless white coveralls were stripping the engine cowling. Borja slipped his arm through Tremayne's and led him across to an iron door set in the nearest wall. Their footsteps echoed hollowly on the stone floor.

"You realize that it would be futile for you to attempt an escape," Borja said.

But Tremayne hadn't been thinking of attempting an escape. Certainly not before he met the man who had masterminded this operation. He'd wait and assess his chances after he had learned a little more about this place.

The arc lights clamped onto platforms at the corners of the chamber were powerful. Tremayne could feel their heat, yet strangely enough, they weren't oppressive. He could also feel a cooling current of air and, looking up, saw the air-conditioning vents placed at intervals along the walls. He noted their position.

"This fortress is quite inaccessible," Borja was telling him. "There is only one other exit and that connects the mountain with the village you saw as we came in. There is no fear of being disturbed—the natives here believe that the mountain is haunted by evil spirits, a superstition we naturally encourage. We are not bothered. The occasional person who does happen to blunder across our path—a fisherman, perhaps, seeking shelter from a storm—is simply not seen again. Most effective."

They were almost at the door. "A word of warning, Mr. Battersby." Borja stopped. "Dominat is an extremely sensitive man. I advise you to be cooperative, or the results will be most unpleasant."

Tremayne didn't reply.

As they reached the door, there was a whirring sound and the thick iron door slid back into the wall. Above the door, Tremayne noticed a tiny aperture and guessed that the place was rigged with closed-circuit television.

They were in a small steel-lined room. Borja turned back and stood facing the wall through which they had just entered. Then, sensing the movement more than feeling it, Tremayne realized they were standing in some sort of an elevator. The wall opened and they stepped out into another room.

Tremayne blinked. For a moment he thought he was in the chrome-plated vulgarity of a modern hotel.

The room was huge; its walls were hung with ceiling-high flame-colored curtains, and on the floor was a wall-to-wall carpet of some writhing pattern so vivid it made Tremayne wince. But if tasteless, the carpet was deep-piled, and as he followed Borja, it felt as if he were walking on a sponge.

"Keep behind me," Borja warned.

Tremayne obeyed. He noted the absence of guards. One thing was sure—no one thought he had a hope in hell of getting out.

Borja stopped again. His nervousness seemed to be returning. He took out a handkerchief and wiped at his forehead, even though the place was air-conditioned. Feeling a cynical satisfaction through his own apprehension, Tremayne walked on, toward a door at the end of the room that looked as if it were coated with gold plate. Suddenly, without warning, a high shrill note sounded, splitting the silence, and in both of Tremayne's ears there jolted abruptly a pain as if his ear drums were being drilled with red-hot gimlets.

He reeled as if he had been clubbed, clapping his hands over his tortured ears. A hand grabbed his arm and jerked him back. The thin screaming ceased, and gradually as Tremayne shook his dazed head the pain in his ears subsided.

"You fool!" Borja snarled. "I told you to keep behind me. Another few seconds and you would have been deafened for life."

"For God's sake," Tremayne panted. "What was it?"

"Ultrahigh-frequency sound, triggered by your body."

Borja was squinting at him. Tremayne nodded. "Oh, of course. I've never experienced it at such intensity, and never before as a protective measure."

"A shaft like that could penetrate into your brain and shatter it to pieces. Now perhaps you will do as you are told."

Borja veered left to a fluted column, a pseudo-Doric

attempt that looked ludicrous against the hideous carpet flowing around its base. He seemed nervous again, or else satisfied that Tremayne had learned his lesson; in any case he made no attempt to cover up the position of the small button he pressed.

For a moment nothing happened, then one leaf of that huge double door at the end of the room swung open.

"Come on." Borja's voice was not so suave as usual. Careful to keep behind, Tremayne followed him through the doorway and into another room.

The next room was almost identical to the first. And the next. Since the plane had been slid into the side of the mountain they had passed through seven doors.

He looked around him in astonishment. It was more like a ballroom, one of the hugest rooms he had ever seen. Moorish pillars and frescoes, gaudily colored divans and cushions, incense-burning pots on gold-plated tripods, bowls of fruit and flagons of wine, all striving for the expression of voluptuous and sensual pleasure. To the Englishman's aesthetic eye the effect was grotesque.

His glance had settled on some weird gleaming gadgetry to one side of the room near its far end when Tremayne detected movement there. His eyes flickered to it. A man was rising from behind a huge metallic desk.

He was dressed in a white blouse open right down to his waist, and as he rose to his full height, the desk silently swiveled to one side so that he could walk straight from his aluminum chair.

Tremayne studied him, at first with wonder and then with respect. The agent was lean—stringy almost—but he was over six feet tall. Still he had to look up at this man.

"Good afternoon. Welcome to my fortress."

The voice was expectedly deep and vibrant. He halted in front of Tremayne and crossed his bare forearms. The muscles writhed like hawsers. He was a colossus, and he emanated a magnetic aura of tremendous force. This acted like an irritant on the Englishman.

"Borja's been telling me about you," he said, his face composed but with a studied negligence, almost insolence, in his voice. "The scientific genius with a yen for the macabre."

Tremayne's boxing body waited for one of those great fists to move. But Dominat just laughed; he even looked pleased.

Borja spoke quickly. "This is Charles Battersby, the physicist I told you about. A brilliant man, but rather uncooperative. Perhaps you can make him change his mind."

Tremayne studied Dominat's face. It was handsome and intelligent. His eyes flickered and there was a gleam behind them that suggested distant lightning.

But apart from the man's tremendous physique it was Dominat's voice that impressed Tremayne. It was cultured and, except for its slight lilt, could have been an upper-class English voice.

Dominat seemed to divine his thoughts. "I am an Oxford man, Mr. Battersby," he said, turning his back on Borja. "Balliol College."

Tremayne nodded. There was no point in explaining that he, too, had received an Oxford education. After all, this wasn't really meant to be an Old Boys' Reunion. Though perhaps if he did tell Dominat he was an Oxford man, it might give him an advantage in the undefined future. "Yes, I was there myself."

Dominat smiled strangely. "That is most interesting. We must compare notes while you are working here. Do you like Omar Khayyám, Mr. Battersby?"

Tremayne was taken aback. "Well, yes, I . . ."

Dominat nodded. "Omar the Tentmaker. I have so little opportunity to discuss such things, surrounded as I am by . . . technicians."

Still ignoring Borja who was standing in the center of the floor, Dominat walked across to one side of the room. Tremayne watched as his spatulate thumb flicked down a switch.

"Mr. Battersby. Come here."

Steel shutters separated silently. It was a window to the world. Tremayne looked down the shining lava slope, two thousand feet down to the green jungly sea. Softly, with a menace in his voice that reminded Tremayne of steel slithering from a scabbard, Dominat said:

"You are in the belly of Morne au Diable. This room is a man-made cavern. There are scores like it. Rooms and tunnels and shafts bored by atomic tools, my tools." He wheeled and pointed back into the room. "Look over here."

Following Dominat's outstretched arm, Tremayne saw that he was pointing at a weird contraption he had noticed before when he first entered the room.

"Borja!"

Normally Tremayne would have been delighted at the way the Spaniard scuttled across the room, but he had suddenly sensed that Dominat was playing with him as a cat plays with a mouse. He watched apprehensively.

Borja fitted himself in between what looked like metal caricatures of two human legs and arms. They were jointed, and stood vertically side by side. Each "hand," reaching above Borja's head, ended in a huge, two-pronged metal claw. Now Borja had pressed his legs sideways, fitting his thighs into clips on the shiny steel uprights, and then, lifting his arms, he did the same with his wrists. He stood there as if bound to two queer posts.

"One hand," Dominat said.

Borja seemed to make no real effort. He bent his right arm. The metal "arm" bent with it. The claw arched down and now Tremayne saw on the floor an iron weight shaped like a giant circular cheese. Borja's fingers moved and the claw hooked its pincers through the ring on the top of the iron.

Tremayne's eyes widened in astonishment. Again with seemingly no effort, Borja lifted the weight. His body straightened and then he stood there, smiling crookedly at Tremayne's bewildered face, while from the claw just above his own hand there dangled a mass of metal which should have ripped his arm from its socket.

Dominat nodded at the Englishman, smiling.

"Two tons," he said. "Two tons of solid iron. Lifted with one arm."

"Good God," Tremayne said involuntarily. "How?"

"Advanced cybernetics. My little monster is so designed that every muscular movement of its user is amplified enormously. It gives a man the power of a giant. It is unique. There is nothing like it anywhere. Yet this is only one item in an arsenal of tools I have perfected here."

"Very clever," Tremayne conceded, "but I've seen similar gimmicks."

Even this backhanded compliment brought a glow of pleasure to the giant's eyes. Tremayne suspected Dominat's lust for recognition and power was driven by a pitiful inferiority complex. While Dominat had an audience for his toys, at least Tremayne was safe.

"All right, Borja," Dominat said, "over here."

The Spaniard disconnected himself from the metal frame and came at once. He stood waiting nervously.

"Sit down, Mr. Battersby," Dominat invited pleasantly. "You seem interested in my handyman. I call it 'Titan.'"

Dominat looked speculatively down at Tremayne for a moment before he went on. "I maintain the prime requirement of science is honesty. One may fool himself, but not the elemental laws. As a brilliant physicist, Battersby, you'll agree with this?"

"I suppose so," said Tremayne, whose physics was actually about high school standard.

Dominat looked at him curiously for a moment, then he clasped his hands behind his back in a lecturing pose.

"In Titan's metal I have used a combination of the derivatives of the olefins, the acetylenes and the polymethylenes—the latter, of course"—he smiled—"being a branch of the cyclanes."

Tremayne nodded with pursed lips.

"But the first two groups will combine to form compounds only by the replacement of some of their atoms. This, Battersby, was my main problem. It took almost two years to solve. But now—" Dominat grinned, as if he were enjoying himself "—now I have succeeded in combining the olefin C-two H-four directly with bromine to form an additive compound, ethylene dibromide. And there," he ended triumphantly, pointing to the gleaming contraption, "is the result."

"Brilliant," murmured Tremayne. "Quite extraordinary."

Dominat turned and took a few paces. When he came back he was smiling, but somehow nothing happened to his eyes. He halted.

"Borja," he said suddenly, "you are even a worse bungler than I thought."

"What!"

"This man is no physicist. Are you?" he demanded of Tremayne.

Tremayne at last was glad to say it. "Well, I know about Newton and the apple. That seemed to be enough to fool poor old Borja. I've met types like him before—brilliant academically, but not endowed with a great deal of common sense. In fact, I'm surprised you've teamed up with him."

But it seemed Dominat was more than academically brilliant. "Your disruptive purpose is plain to me, Battersby. It won't work." Borja relaxed back on the luridly covered divan. Dominat did not look at him. "Let us return to you. I thought you were a fake; any physicist would have known the elementary principles of my Titan, if not the finer cybernetic points. But you obviously had never heard of cybernetics. Just as obviously your knowledge of chemistry is as limited as that of physics. In describing how Titan works, I gave you nothing more or less than a technical description of the formation of hydrocarbons. Titan is made of stainless steel. You are caught out, Mr. Battersby. Now perhaps you will tell me your real name."

Tremayne hesitated, then told him.

Dominat repeated the name thoughtfully, but it didn't seem to mean anything to him.

"And you are working for whom?"

That, Tremayne wasn't going to tell him.

Dominat's smile broadened. "It doesn't really matter. I know that you're an agent and you know you have to die."

"And the real Battersby?" Dominat asked, as Borja opened his mouth to speak. "You were acting as a cover for him, is that right?"

Tremayne shrugged, but didn't reply. By now, he hoped, the real Charles Battersby was safely back in London.

Dominat walked across to the now visibly quaking Borja and stood over him. "As for you, Borja," he began menacingly, "you failed to bring the plasma beam to a state of perfection, then hand it over to me. Not only have you lost the core of the nuclear reactor, but the physicist you kidnapped to assist you with your work turns out to be a fake. Who he happens to be working for at the moment is of no consequence—the point is, he's working as an agent." He held up his hand to forestall Borja. "Oh, I know about Hood. I have already made arrangements to have him eliminated."

Tremayne's heart sank. There was no way to warn Hood that his life was in danger. If it wasn't already too late.

Fortunately," Dominat continued, "Sugarstrike has now been brought forward so that it will be set in operation at midnight tomorrow. We will be hampered to only a minor extent by the loss of the plasma beam, since we needed it only to throw those vessels of the United States fleet stationed in these waters into momentary confusion, to give us cover for our attack. It was also to provide us with necessary finance. But now that it is gone, we must work as well as we can with what we have."

Tremayne realized that Dominat was playing with Borja as he had played with "Battersby." There was that mocking undercurrent in his voice as well as the distant gleam in his eyes.

"Which brings me to the unfortunate part. Don Pedro,

my elegant little Spanish grandee, I'm afraid your usefulness has come to an end."

Borja gulped and Tremayne could actually see what little color there was left in his face drain away. His hands fluttered feebly by his side. Dominat laughed. "Yes, you are a clever scientist, but otherwise a fool. You were too easily deceived."

Borja was on his feet. He faced the giant angrily.

"Just a minute," Borja said. "All right, I was deceived. But that had nothing to do with the experiment's failure. This man was with me in my boat, helpless. The other fellow, his colleague named Hood, was responsible. Tremayne and his false identity had no bearing on what happened."

With the daring of a man who had nothing to lose, Tremayne said:

"I'm afraid you're wrong there, old chap. My friend got on to you because I told him about the atomic-powered destroyer you were after. And I was able to tell him because you conveniently allowed me access to your radio transmitter in the house on Little Cayman. Sorry, chum, but you were the bunny all along. If anything happens to Hood you'll have to answer to a force much stronger than yours."

Face smiling, body tensed in his chair, Tremayne waited for Dominat to turn angrily on him. Nothing happened. The giant's attention was all for his partner.

He walked in a leisurely manner to a long narrow cupboard against one wall—the sort of compartment which might be expected to hold billiard cues, Tremayne thought. Dominat turned with his hand on the doorknob. He smiled back at Tremayne, a thin stretching of his lips that showed perfect white teeth.

"I hope you will be patient with my little indulgence."

He wrenched open the cupboard door. His hand darted in, came out.

"Mother of Jesus," Tremayne heard Borja whisper. "No!"

Dominat turned and came back. Tremayne's scalp

tingled. The man was holding a great bull whip. He gripped the handle in his right hand and through his left the thick plaited hide was slowly drawn until in his palm lay the tapered end—to Tremayne's fascinated eyes the end of the whip seemed to be a trace of thin steel, pliable as soft leather.

"The door is open, Borja," Dominat said, softly again. "Through it, and you are safe."

"No!"

"Very well."

Dominat turned his back and began to walk slowly toward his desk, apparently to give himself distance for the whip's great length.

"Run, you fool!" Tremayne hissed. "He'll keep his word."

Borja hesitated, staring at the giant's back, his face ashen with fear.

"Run!"

And Borja ran.

He leaped round the end of the divan and jumped over a pile of cushions, his feet making quick sharp slapping sounds on the polished parquetry of the floor as with desperate haste they took him toward the door. And Tremayne, his eyes compulsively on Dominat, saw the colossus turn, casually raise his right hand upward and back, and then snap it forward.

Like a striking snake, faster than a snake, the dreadful length uncoiled itself and lashed across the room, the steel trace glinting silvery. There was a crack like a gunshot. Borja halted as if he had run into a wall. His head and his body arched back. Then his head lolled sideways and his body sagged to the floor, to lie there twitching a little while the mess spread slowly.

Tremayne was a man of hard, often harsh, experience. Yet as Borja fell he swung his head away; unable even with his experience to look at a man with his neck cut halfway through. He looked at the floor and his stomach churned.

Dominat flicked the end of the whip back into his

hand. He wiped the trace with a handkerchief, then walked to his desk where he pressed a button in a small console. In the wall behind the desk a door slid sideways silently. A figure stepped through.

"The disintegrator, Mero," Dominat said casually.

At his voice Tremayne looked up. He saw ugliness. The face was Creole, pockmarked and distorted into what seemed to be a permanent grimace. The body was hunchbacked. The powerful hands hung listlessly down by his side. They were very large hands. In answer to the order Mero grunted. He showed no reaction at all to the mess on the floor a few feet from the doorway.

"Mero unfortunately cannot speak," Dominat explained to his visitor. "A congenital defect. This is Mr. Tremayne, Mero. He will be staying with us for a while."

Mero's low-slung head did not move but his pale eyes slanted upward to Tremayne's face as he lifted Borja's limp bulk easily and slung it over one shoulder. He left the room.

Walking back to the whip cupboard Dominat said:

"The body will now be placed in our nuclear disintegrator. One flick of the switch, a flash of light, and then —pouf—nothing. Not one single trace of our erstwhile friend will remain. Perhaps you would be interested to see how it works."

Dominat sprawled his great body on a divan and lit a cigarette.

"Yes, I think you should spend some time here, Tremayne," he said, nodding so that the thick plume of exhaled smoke wriggled in the air. "Can you imagine why?"

So that you can have the satisfaction of seeing me squirm, Tremayne thought. He had nothing to say, except disgusted and pointless curses. He looked at Dominat's calm handsome face, so that he would not have to look at the dark stain near the door.

"It will be pleasant to have the company of a cultured mind," Dominat said. "My men here are brilliant technicians, as you can imagine from what you've already seen, yet philosophically and intellectually their minds are deserts, I'm afraid. Perhaps I shall show you some more of my little inventions, maybe even my *pièce de résistance*. Even to a nonscientist this will be fascinating. Considering," Dominat said soberly, "that its possession could tip the balance of world power."

CHAPTER

FIVE

~~~~~~~~~~~~~~~~~~~~~~~~~~~~~~~~

"GOD DAMN IT, Hood, stop playing games with me," Fortescue roared. "I'm a busy man. And I've never had much time for poetry."

Hood couldn't refrain from smiling. His superior, Fortescue, certainly was not the type who read poetry. Hood lifted the receiver an inch from his ear and tried to get an image of the red-faced Englishman sitting at his desk in the headquarters office of Intertrust—a man who seemed to personify the unimaginative blustering type of British senior officer. Yet, Hood knew, Fortescue's manner was deceptive. Behind his blue protuberant eyes there was a brain that was as keen as the edge of a razor blade. There would need to be, as Fortescue and his American counterpart, Blair, were solely responsible for the English-speaking segment of the top-secret, interpower, nuclear security organization—Intertrust.

Hood's call to Geneva had been put through immediately. There was no delay. There never was. A top-secret scrambling apparatus installed in a back room of Government House spewed out the words in a tangle of gibberish—words which, at the other end of the line, were sorted back into their proper sequence.

When Fortescue spoke again his voice was a shade softer. "I think we shall have to write Tremayne off completely. Even if they don't kill him straight away, after all he has been through, his efficiency will be impaired."

"Maybe," said Hood shortly.

"Whatever has happened to him, I don't want you turning this thing into a personal crusade. This department is not motivated by feelings of revenge. Remember that."

Hood was tired. He hadn't yet been back to the villa on Windward Road where he and Tremayne had been staying. He was hungry and needed a long, long sleep.

"Hood, there's something we want you to look into. It might mean nothing, but as you're already on the spot you're to find out what you can. A report from Washington indicates there might be something of a nuclear buildup in the Caribbean area. This could tie in with a recent concentration of rabble-rousers in the Caribbean. The troublemakers from smaller nations Intertrust keeps an eye on have all suddenly decided to head for the Trinidad area—then they seem to have vanished into thin air. The buildup area appears to be based somewhere in the Windward Islands. That's all we know. No one is claiming any responsibility for it. Scout around and see what you can find. Okay?"

"It could tie in with the Borja affair," Hood murmured. "Sugarstrike. Does that mean anything to you?"

"It could mean anything. You'll need a man with you, I guess. I'll send Murimoto out to you on the next flight. Meet him at the airport. And keep in touch, Hood."

From Government House Hood took a taxi back to the villa on Windward Road. After fixing himself a belated breakfast, he took a shower, then, clad only in his shorts, he padded into the kitchen, where he mixed himself a long cool drink.

Murimoto was a good man. The best, he reflected as he sipped his drink. It wasn't strong enough. He splashed a little more rum into it.

Murimoto was an asset to have on any job. He was normally only used for special action work when his particular skills were required. His cover was the International Club in Geneva where he worked as a gym instructor.

A small inoffensive-looking Japanese, he had taught Mark Hood all he knew about the gentle art of karate. No doubt Fortescue knew how Hood respected Murimoto's Oriental wisdom. Maybe the old boy thought he was about to do something rash about trying to find Tremayne. Well, it suited them both to have Murimoto sent down here.

Walking out onto the wide veranda, Hood unraveled his length into a canvas beach chair. Beyond the lawn and the dirt road that bordered the beach, the blue sea looked cool and inviting. As he watched it a strange lethargy crept over him. The sky was a bright blue and there was not a cloud in it. His eyelids were getting heavier and he tried to keep his mind on the events of the past few hours.

There were too many loose ends. Ignoring Fortescue and his vague instructions about rabble-rousers and nuclear stockpiling, he concentrated on the discovery he had made in Borja's boat. There was something that didn't click and he was sure it was embodied on the sheet of rice paper he had found in the brown leather folder—the heading, Sugarstrike, and the words "I rose and on the throne of Satan sate."

The meaning still eluded him. He concentrated on the heading, Sugarstrike.

Strike had an aggressive, biting ring to it and, of course, Borja and his associates were definitely planning something. Now, *Sugar*. Sugar. Hood sipped his drink. Sugar. It could mean anything. Sugarstrike. Strike. Sugar grew in profusion all over this area. Jamaica, Cuba.

He banged his fist down so violently on the table beside him that his drink was upset. The glass rolled over on its side and the spilled liquor formed a steady drip onto the floor. Of course. Why hadn't he seen it before? It was so simple. Too simple. Like the story of the purloined letter, he thought, the solution was so obvious that no one had even considered it.

He scooped his clothes up from the bathroom floor and dressed again. The Jaguar he had rented as soon as he and Tremayne arrived in Jamaica was outside in the garage.

"Cuba, sir."

"Hood, what *is* this?" Fortescue was angry. "What do you mean by wasting my time as well as tying up an important telephone connection, not to mention the charges? I'm a busy man."

But Hood knew his chief. He was undeterred. "Sugarstrike, sir. My guess is that whatever it is that's brewing will be aimed at Cuba and if that number—five-three—does happen to be the date, then there's no time to lose."

"What are you talking about?" Fortescue boomed.

"Look at it this way, sir. Cuba. With its alliances and so close to the United States, Cuba is in a very strategic situation."

Hood." Fortescue spoke with icy calm. "This is a

smoothly functioning intergovernmental body. We have at our disposal almost unlimited resources of experts whose job it is to evaluate what people like you—field workers—send in." Suddenly Fortescue laughed. "Cuba, you might be interested to know, was the very first possibility that sprang to mind. Now, leave all the deciphering to us and follow your instructions. Get some rest; then, when you meet Murimoto at the airport tonight, I want you both to get cracking and see what you can learn about the movements of those boys Washington is worrying about."

On the way back to the villa Hood felt chastened, like a schoolboy who has been caught out in something. Okay, he told himself, he would get some sleep.

But not yet.

He had a visitor.

The girl was sitting in the wide, cool room that opened onto the veranda. She had mixed herself a drink and was delicately sipping at it. As Hood entered she looked up at him with dark, wide, hungry eyes. "You've been a long time," she said.

"Maybe I'd have been back sooner," Hood said, "if I'd known you were waiting. Who are you, anyway?"

The girl laughed, throwing her head back and displaying a row of even white teeth. "My name is Jane."

Hood moved across to the bar and turned so that as he mixed himself a drink he could keep his eyes on her.

His unexpected visitor was a dusky, scarlet-lipped beauty. From her ears dangled two large gold rings. Her low-cut red dress, which seemed to be fighting a losing battle to keep her breasts concealed, clung possessively to her full, ripe body. She stood up and crossed the floor to where Hood was standing. She held out her empty glass. "I'll have the same as you're having," she said.

Hood handed her her drink. "What else do you want?" he asked.

"I want you."

"I beg your pardon?"

"I said, I want you."

He didn't trust her. He was sure this was a trap, but the approach was so unsubtle. She laughed again. "I see you don't understand me. I saw you this morning." She gestured vaguely toward the beach. "I saw you on the veranda. What I saw interested me, Mr.—Mr. . . ."

"Call me Mark."

"Mark." She savored the word. "Mark. I like that."

"And?"

"And so I said to myself, 'Jane, honey, why don't you carve off a slice from that great big hunk of meat?' I'll admit I'm a greedy girl, Mark."

Hood finished his drink. "Well, it's a woman's world."

She ran the tips of her fingers lightly down his arm. The skin shivered in their wake. "When I came out of the water and up here, you were out. I decided to wait."

The hunger was raging in her eyes. Hood had seen it before and he recognized it for what it was. He understood. Desire. Not ordinary desire, but a desire so cruel it was a sickness. She was a nymphomaniac.

"Mark," she breathed urgently.

As she caressed him, he could feel the desire well up in his own body. It became stronger. He kissed her. Her lips tasted of salt. He bit into her lower lip until the blood ran and she squealed with pain, then he led her into the bedroom.

The first time was too quick, but the girl proved her ability in arousing Hood's libido. She was experienced, and he was overwhelmed by a strong feeling of poignancy that amounted almost to a physical pain. It was an unaccustomed feeling and he was reminded of the maxim that each act of love was, in itself, a little death.

Jane ran her hand lightly across his chest. "Thank you, Mark," she whispered. "Thank you."

It was while they were making love the second time that she tried to kill him.

"Just a minute," Hood grunted. His left elbow was resting on the lower edge of a pillow, which was inconvenient. He lifted his elbow and rolled his upper body to the right. And so instead of digging into his vertebrae and severing the spinal cord, the needled point of the stiletto she had in her right hand simply grazed down his side, was deflected by a rib, and dug into the mattress.

CHAPTER

SIX

"YOU BITCH," Hood said softly.

Beautiful eyes glared hotly up into his, but this time not with sexual desire. She tugged the blade clear. She twisted her hand around and lunged the point at his throat. But even with their bodies so close it was easy for him to flick her wrist aside. Then, fairly gently, Hood clipped her into unconsciousness with his fist.

What a way to die, he thought ironically, what a time. And then he thought what a stupid damn position to be in, lying there protecting her but with his own back wide open. He rolled sideways and hit the floor in the *kiba dachi* stance; listening, eyes on the closed door, waiting.

Nothing happened. Quietly and quickly he pulled on his shorts and trousers. Suddenly, sharply, he uttered a long cry of simulated pain, and at once he darted to the side of the door.

He had just got there when the door opened. A change of weapons this time. He saw the revolver barrel poking cautiously through the half-open door. Even as his right hand chopped down in a controlled *shuto* for the man's neck, Hood's left arm snaked out, so that he caught him around the throat as he slumped forward, and lowered him quietly to the floor.

Hood took the gun. It was heavy, a British Army Webley .45. He did not wait. Believing that any others would be also near the door, knowing he had the advantage of surprise, he leaped out into the passage. His eyes darted to right and left. No one was there, nothing. Either they were running out of assassins or else they believed the girl would be sufficient.

Hood went back in and locked the door. In the sun-washed room, in the center of the rumpled bed, lying there on her back, she looked tantalizingly desirable. It was hard to believe that she had just tried to kill him. But she had waited until he had satisfied her. He bound both of them with strips from a sheet, then dumped the Jamaican on the bed beside her. As an afterthought he gagged them, so that teeth could not be used to pry loose his knots, and then finally he took up the bedroom extension phone. The voice he wanted answered almost at once.

"Hello, Dick," Hood said. "Got a job for you."

"Where are you?" Owen wanted to know.

"At the villa—on Windward Road."

"All right. What happened?"

Hood told him. "I'm tired of being a damn pincushion. Maybe now that the unholy bastards know you're in on it I might get some peace. But I don't want to get otherwise involved, Dick."

"An attempted murder? I suppose you won't mind filing a charge?" the inspector said drily.

"That'll be okay. Better get a car out here."

"Hold on a minute." Hood heard orders being given, then: "My men are on the way. Hang around. You can explain it all when I get there."

"Wilco," said Hood. "I'm not going anywhere except bed, when you get the bodies off it."

It was early evening when Hood awoke. He had had a good long sleep, so deep that when he awoke it took him a moment to remember where he was and what had happened.

He was perspiring. All the windows and doors had been secured against the possibility of another attack. Owen had been persuaded to leave a man patrolling the grounds. "Just in case they try again," Hood had explained. "And I do need the shut-eye."

He glanced at his watch, then, crossing to the telephone, dialed the airport. Murimoto's flight wouldn't be arriving for another three hours.

He was beginning to feel restless. Now that he was refreshed he chafed at the idea of idling away even three hours. He hated being placed in the position where he had to wait.

More to give himself something to do than anything else, he mixed himself a drink.

It was getting cooler outside. A slight breeze wafted up from the sea, bringing with it the heady tang of salt. Hood sat out on the veranda nursing the cool drink in his hands and looking out to sea.

It was as if a drape of the smoothest velvet was being drawn across the sky. The night was beginning to throb, to pulsate, with the sounds of insects, the surf on the

beach, and farther off, the intrusive sounds of the city.
As he laid his head against the back of the chair and
stared up at the sky Hood could feel some of his tension
easing.

He thought about Tremayne, which saddened him.
Then he told himself he was being stupid. He was acting
as if he really believed Tremayne to be dead. If only he
had a clue, a definite trace of Tommy's whereabouts.
Something definite. White or black, nothing indetermi-
nate. It was the not knowing that was working its cor-
rosive influence.

And this new assignment. Could it tie in with Borja's
plans? By the time he had tracked down the rabble-
rousers who were worrying Washington and followed up rumors about the nuclear stockpile, it might be
too late to stop whatever game Borja and his gang were
playing. There was that business of the date. Tomorrow.

A beautiful night. The moon was three-quarters full
and cast a broad shimmering swath across the still
sea. The stars were beginning to show. How far away it
all seemed, Hood thought. How was it possible to equate
such a perfumed, singing night and all the beautiful
things in the world with cold brutal violence, whole-
sale slaughter, and sordid ambition? How? He looked up
at the stars and they seemed to be winking at him.

He started to name the stars. There were Mars—an
easy one, that; Venus. He tried to place the others—
what were their names again? Uranus, Pluto. Jupiter.
And the one that had what looked like a plate around it.
Saturn.

He was still looking up when his mouth dropped open.
His body was rigid.

Saturn.

That was it.

Damn, why hadn't he thought of it before?

He knew now the meaning of the cryptic sentence he
had found in the cabin of the *Barracuda*.

Like the movable scenery in a theater, the night of

beauty was rolled to one side and the stage was set for the other world, the world of evil.

As he watched Murimoto walking across the tarmac toward him Hood was repeating the lines over beneath his breath.

"Good evening, Mark."

Hood's face relaxed into a smile. Standing before him, his little almond eyes gleaming with pleasure, was a rather short Japanese, yet not small; squat, rather, with a bull neck and barn-door shoulders.

"Murimoto. Great to have you along."

After this business was over, Hood thought, as they pushed their way out through the crowded entrance and around to the parking lot where he had left the rented Jag, Murimoto could give him a workout to get his body into needle-sharp fighting trim.

There would be special diets, exercises; then the master would take him through most of the forms and techniques of karate—not even a black belt second dan knew them all—through *uke* and *mawashi uke* and *pinan* (right up to Form Four) and *saifa* and the deadly *seienchen,* then into the defensive techniques of *ippon kumite*. For hour after hour he would be obliged to practice kicking and jumping, throwing his opponent over his shoulder and between his legs, striking with his palm edge, his bunched fist, the heel of his hand and with his elbow in the forceful *hiji uchi*.

But all this would come later. As they drove into the city Hood gave the Japanese a brief rundown on what had happened.

"I'm onto something, I'm sure of it," he said, glancing down at his companion's hands, at the calluses along the edges of his palms. For a couple of hundred times every day for about twenty years those hands had punched a *makiwara* stick, and heaven help anyone who got into the way of them.

". . . and it wasn't until this evening when I—" Hood broke off suddenly.

They were passing through the intersection of East Queen and High Holborn. Hood should have given way to the low black Ferrari which came at him from Holborn; he should not have been talking so much. Only the honed reflexes of the karateist and the experienced hands of the sports car racing driver had the Ferrari whipping past close astern instead of slamming into the Jag's midriff.

"Hell, that was close."

Past the intersection Hood straightened the Jag and backed off on the throttle. In the mirror he saw headlights cutting a swift swath of brilliance as the other car was reefed around to follow.

His brain reacted with the incalculable velocity of thought. That was no chance meeting, that car was meant to ram them; to maim if not to kill, to keep him here.

"Don't these bastards ever give up?" Hood growled, and whipped the stubby gear lever into second. "Tighten your seat belt."

There were close to three hundred horses available in the engine and Hood gave them full rein. The cunning tread of the Pirelli tires bit into the asphalt but did not spin. The Jag surged forward and kept on increasing speed.

Luckily, they were out of East Queen and into Victoria Avenue, with Windward Road, leading to the villa, coming up. There were still bars and restaurants, but not so many. The streets were comparatively empty. At ninety Hood slipped through into fourth gear and held his foot down. Beside him, his face impassive and his body braced, Murimoto sat silently.

Hood knew the Ferrari had the legs of him; he had raced one not so long before in Macao. But was that driver so skilled? His only chance lay in the possibility that he was not.

It looked a slim possibility.

Hood whipped in front of an approaching car with inches to spare, hearing the blast of an angry horn, seeing in his mirror the Ferrari hanging on like a limpet, as if attached by an invisible wire. The Jag was a lovely vehicle, with independent suspension all around and four-wheel powered disc brakes, but she was a family sports sedan, not a racer like that black bullet astern. Hood knew that on the long straight stretch of Windward Road he would be caught.

He did something about that.

A car turning left ahead of him showed him the road leading off Victoria. Hood heel-and-toed the pedals, feet and hands moving in synchronized speed. The Jag came down into second with a throaty snarl as he drifted her into the corner—and into a set of approaching headlights. Down went the accelerator pedal. A plug missing, the slightest falter in those sounding pistons, and they would be head-on into disaster. There was no miss. The big motor got its coal and responded valiantly, taking its streamlined body in a shaving slice across the radiator of the approaching car. Hood straightened the wheel and went up to third. His eyes flickered to the mirror. There, in an even tighter turn, a fraction slower, and taking a second longer to pick up speed, came the Ferrari. And at one hundred miles an hour seconds mean saving yards. Hood knew that with a few more sharp turns he could get back onto Windward Road with enough gained to reach the villa safely. Once there, he and this silent man beside him might maintain the advantage.

Half a mile, another intersection. This was clear of the downtown section, an area of darkened villas. Hood took her in a fast right-hand sweep and bulleted down the straight approach. He had not shifted from third when the next intersection was on him. To the right again, now heading back toward Windward Road. Now left into the wide main road and he pressed her up through the gears until she was at peak revs in fourth. One second . . . another . . . three, before the bright white swath of following lights showed astern. The Jag howled at her utmost power.

"Got a gun?" Hood shouted to Murimoto.

"No."

He should have known. This was a man who could kick a gun from a hand before the trigger finger could take up the first pressure. Providing he got close enough. . . .

"We'll be there soon. Unclip your belt now. You make for the gate and wait just inside the hedge. I'll do what I can with the thirty-eight, then join you. Stand by."

For the moment Hood had forgotten that he was advising a master of tactics, but Murimoto merely said, "Very well," and undid his safety belt. And whipped out a saving hand just in time against the dash as Hood used the brake pedal. The pads on each disc gripped viselike and clawed her to a swift smooth stop. Murimoto was out and through the gate in two leaps. Hood flicked off all lights, then ran around in front of the hood and crouched there, the .38 lined up with the left-hand fender.

The full-powered snarl first, cutting through the quiet moonlit night, then the lights; and the grinding grip of similar claws and a black body snaking in to a fierce stop just ahead of the Jag. That was a damn fool place to pull in, Hood thought momentarily, unless there were a lot of them; then the Ferrari was backing, threatening to pin him against the radiator, and he was leaping for its driver's door, surprised as he went to see only one figure silhouetted through the rear window. As the Ferrari halted a foot in front of its quarry Hood had the door open, using it as protection for his lower body, his gun hand clear.

"Hold it right there," he ordered.

There was a pause. Hood smelled something, and was astonished but his caution remained unimpaired. And then a voice said:

"What sort of a damn fool game is this? You nearly killed me back there. What d'you mean to do? Make sure of it?"

"Out," Hood ordered. "Slow and easy now, hands in view all the time."

"With pleasure." A seductive rustling, something shapely in the moonlight, then his victim was standing before him. "I got the license number but I just had to meet the maniac who was driving."

Hood finished his inspection of the car's interior and came back to its driver. He saw an attractive slim girl clad in a bikini that left her 99 percent visible. He had not long since left something similar; he remained careful.

"You're American," he said.

"That's right."

"Why did you chase us?"

"I told you. You damn near skewered me. I meant to catch you and let you know just how I feel about that. Oh, put that silly thing away. What are you, a gangster or something?"

Hood pocketed his weapon. Once or twice his life had depended on people not knowing about that back holster.

"I'm a private investigator," he said.

"Uh-uh," she said, shaking her head. "Now I know."

"Fine. Who are you?"

"You're no private eye," she still evaded him. "You're Mark Hood. And I tried to catch *you!*"

"You damn near did."

"Thank you, sir. You still don't know me?"

"Should I?"

"Thank you for nothing. I drove in last year's Monte Carlo Rally. I saw you there."

Tommy Tremayne had often commented on the weight of Hood's gallantry.

"I would have remembered if I'd seen you."

"Is that a compliment?" she asked. "I'm Mona Gillespie."

There had been an M. Gillespie driving at Monte Carlo, Hood remembered. After all, you didn't get to meet all the entrants. . . .

"Right now I could use a drink," she said.

He smiled at her. "Come on in and I'll fix you one."

Mona was passing through the gate when she jumped

almost its height and yelped. A ghost had risen and an unghostly hand gripped her arm.

"Mark, quick!"

"It's all right. This is Mr. Murimoto. He's a friend of mine. Miss Gillespie, Murimoto."

"Phew. Any more surprises?"

Walking down the path she turned to Hood. "How come you almost collected me? That's not like the guy who came in second in the rally."

"I guess it was my own fault," Hood admitted. "I was talking too much."

They halted at the door. "Well, I'm glad we met—I was growing bored here. Maybe that's the real reason I gave chase."

Hood opened the door and listened. Murimoto slipped through and switched on the lights.

Working behind the bar, Hood got his first good look at her. The moonlight had revealed her body adequately; now he saw that while her face was not beautiful in the accepted sense, it was attractive in a browned, assured way. She had a look of competence about her. But then she was a first-class driver. She might make a very good friend, Hood thought, encouraged by her beautiful body. She saw him judging it. Hood smiled.

"You always drive undressed like that? Liable to cause accidents."

"I'd just come from the boat. I was on my way downtown for cigarettes."

Murimoto retired discreetly to the opposite side of the room.

They talked, and all the while they were talking, Hood was watching the girl. She was perfectly at ease, sipping her drink and behaving as if they were old friends. Perfectly relaxed.

But then Jane, the girl who had tried to kill him, had also been relaxed. Hood remained on his guard. He noticed that Murimoto had positioned his chair just behind and a little to one side of the divan on which Mona was sitting. Although he seemed at his ease, Hood knew that the Jap was tensed, watching and waiting for the girl to make a false move.

After a while Hood's suspicions lulled. Borja and company wouldn't be so foolish as to try the same trick twice.

Mona was talking. Hood caught at one word and his eyebrows contracted in a puzzled frown.

"Whales?"

Mona laughed. She was smoking a cigarette, delicately holding it between her first and second finger. "It certainly looked like a whale."

"In these waters?" Something was nibbling at Hood's subconscious.

"I wondered myself," Mona replied. "But whales migrate or something, don't they?"

Hood was still frowning. "I don't know that this is the way they come. I wouldn't be sure of that." He glanced at Murimoto. The Jap's face was expressionless. "What did it look like, this thing?"

Mona shrugged. "Like a whale, I guess. That's why I thought it was a whale. It was dark, you see. There was a full moon, but quite a lot of cloud. I was bringing the *Goosewing*—that's my boat—past the northern tip of Dominica when this . . . this object popped up out of the water. It was round, like I'd always imagined a whale to be—not cigar-shaped like a submarine." She shook her head. "Oh, I don't know. It was there and then it wasn't. I mean, I hadn't seen it surfacing. Then it went under and that was all I saw of it."

Hood was strangely excited as if he knew that the final question was about to be answered. It was instinctive, something which could never be explained—like that magic electricity-charged moment when you knew you had finally succeeded in blasting a girl's last defense asunder.

"Did you hear anything? Engines?"

"My own engine. No, I couldn't say."

"Dominica, you say?"

"Just off Devil's Mountain."

"Devil's Mountain?" Hood repeated sharply.

"That's right," Mona said. "It's an extinct volcano."

Hood said:

"This craft of yours. What size is she? I don't suppose you'd charter her for a cruise?"

"Forty feet. Twin diesel. Sleeps six people. But I'm fresh out of crew."

It was a risk, Hood thought, but one he had to take. Then he remembered that there is such a thing as coincidence, and he did recall Mona's name as a rally competitor. Even in his game there were some things you had to accept, and the honesty of Mona Gillespie was one of them.

"Not anymore," Hood said.

"Oh?" Mona arched her eyebrows. And Hood was thinking: The boat would be perfect. How they got off again didn't matter. Apart from Martinique, all of the Windward Islands were British and that meant disciplined police, and governors or consuls. She could leave as soon as she landed them. He would see she got a reliable crew, and he and Murimoto could easily get from island to island.

Mona drained her glass. "Now look, just what am I getting mixed up with here?"

Hood shrugged. "If you're scared let's forget it. Another drink?"

She looked at him levelly. "You'll have to do better than that, Mark. If I'm risking my boat I want to know why."

"How come you run such a boat?" Hood said, prodded into bluntness.

"My father runs a steel corporation."

"The poor little rich girl?"

"Poor be damned. I have myself a great time, thanks."

"But no risks, huh?"

"I'll take a risk when I know what and why!"

"One moment, please," said Murimoto placatingly.

Mona stared at Hood. Suddenly she smiled. "What are we scrapping for?"

This girl was disturbing. Challenging.

Murimoto had stepped forward in front of her. Casually, without self-consciousness, he held out his dreadful hands.

"We need your boat, Miss Gillespie. I assure you Mr. Hood is a man to be trusted. Otherwise," Murimoto ended simply, "I should not be here with him. I hope you believe that."

"I see," said Mona.

Hood glanced at his watch. "Okay. Do we have a deal?"

"If you tell me what it is."

"To take us to the Windward Islands."

"And?"

"That's all."

"Come on. What's happened to all those risks?"

"There may be some danger en route. More, if we waste time."

"What are you after on the Windward Islands?"

"I can't tell you that, but it's important."

She uncurled brown legs and stood up. "Okay, it's a deal."

Hood grinned. "How are your stores?"

"Full. Enough to last the three of us a month. And liquor."

"We'll go easy on that. One more question. How come your crew took a powder?"

Mona shrugged. "They're Jamaicans, hired for the season. Maybe they want to be with Momma, or a rum bottle. Here it's nice ashore."

"Or maybe they don't want to serve under a girl?"

Her eyes flickered at him. "Maybe. How do *you* feel about serving under a girl? Because in my boat you will be."

"I was in the Navy, I'm a disciplined man," Hood said, and smiled, and Murimoto relaxed. "Where's your boat?"

"In the marina at Port Royal. The *Goosewing*. White hull and gray upperworks."

"We'll find her. Now why don't you go back and wait for us? We'll pack and return my car. But don't prepare for sea till we get there. I want a quiet departure. And if any of your crew change their minds and return, get rid of 'em, huh?"

"All right."

Hood nodded. "I'll pay anything in reason."

"I'll settle for a week's driving instruction when we get back."

After the girl had gone, Murimoto asked, "You have found something?"

"Yes," Hood replied, rubbing his hands together. "And with a bit of luck now, I might find out exactly what happened to Tommy Tremayne."

CHAPTER
SEVEN

~~~~~~~~~~~~~~~~~~~~~~

WHILE THEY WERE hurriedly preparing for their departure Hood explained. As he spoke his voice was breathless with barely repressed excitement.

"It came to me tonight, just before you arrived. I knew there was something wrong with that sentence on the slip of paper I found in Borja's boat. Something that didn't quite fit in. 'I rose and on the throne of Satan sate.' Then, when I was looking at the stars, I discovered *how* that quotation is wrong. It really is 'on the throne of *Saturn* sate.' It comes from the *Rubáiyát* of Omar Khayyám. As I remember, the line preceding it goes: 'Up from Earth's center through the seventh gate.' Now do you see?"

But Murimoto was looking at him blankly.

"And then, when Mona just happened to mention Devil's Mountain, the last piece was fitted into place. Devil's Mountain—Satan's throne. An extinct volcano and, as sure as God made little apples, that's where Borja has gone. Through the seventh gate. That probably has a definite significance too. Then there's Mona's whale. I didn't tell you, did I, about the submarine thing that was out at the Serrana Bank just before the *Barracuda* was blown out of the water? It was more like a tank, really, running along the seabed on treads." He shrugged. "Could be we're rushing off on a wild goose chase, but I don't think so. At least it's something to go on—and there's not much time."

A gleam of understanding showed at the corner of Murimoto's bright impenetrable eyes. "Ah so. The Devil in the mountain—Satan—is Borja?"

Hood shook his head. "I'm not sure. I've a hunch Borja wasn't alone in this. Why would he keep that message so carefully—unless it was a message from someone higher up? Maybe someone who'd organized enough resources to accumulate a nuclear stockpile in that area. That ties in, too, with the general exodus of extremist leaders which has thrown Washington into such a stir."

"You think they were summoned to the mountain by the leader, the man who refers to himself as Satan?"

"That's my guess."

They were ready to leave. As they walked toward the front door, Hood placed his arm about Murimoto's shoulder. "It's going to be dangerous," he said.

Murimoto smiled. "I am ready."

"Welcome aboard," Mona greeted them. "I'll show you your berths."

"Let it wait, huh? I'd like to be clear of land by first light."

"If that's what you want."

Hood went on: "Let me handle the navigation. In any case, the Leeward and Windward Islands run in an arc almost from Puerto Rico right down to Trinidad. So long as we head into the rising sun we're bound to run into one of 'em. Now can we get out of here?"

"Cast off." Mona kept her voice low.

Hood did so, letting the supporting float back into the water quietly.

There was a deep-throated roar as the diesels came to life. Mona swung the wheel as the cruiser eased away from the buoy and slipped quietly past the sterns of other sleeping vessels. Then she turned it to port and aimed the craft's nose for the vast gleaming reach of the Caribbean Sea. The wind was astern. They picked up speed.

The phosphorescence creamed away from the *Goose-wing's* bow. The night was mild. Hood looked up again at the stars.

"She handles the boat well," Murimoto said beside him. He had come up so quietly that Hood hadn't heard him.

"Some girl, huh?"

"Indeed. This should be an interesting voyage. Will you tell her the object of our mission?"

Hood glanced over his shoulder to make sure Mona was not within earshot. "Not unless it becomes absolutely necessary. The less she knows what it's all about the better, I think. She can put us off at the island, then wait for us at a safe distance until we return. With Tommy Tremayne, I hope."

Hood swung himself up into the cabin of the cruiser. Mona glanced up at him. "Well?"

"Everything seems to be going very smoothly. Just listen to those engines."

They made a beautiful sound to Hood, who had always admired precision. There was not a single grating beat to their powerful immaculate rhythm.

"When we're out of sight of land," Hood said, "we turn east."

"And?"

"From our position at dawn, Dominica should only be a little south of east."

Mona made a tiny *o* of her mouth. "So it *is* Dominica? I thought it would be."

"What do you mean?" Hood challenged.

She laughed. "I noticed the way your face lit up when I mentioned Devil's Mountain. You *are* going to the mountain, aren't you?"

"Yes."

Hood wasn't sure yet how far he should trust this American girl. If worse came to worst, she would be leading them to Borja and the mysterious Satan and that was a meeting Hood eminently desired. He would learn what had actually happened to Tremayne. He glanced into the compass's dimly lighted face and saw that the heading was south. Looking skyward again he found Polaris.

"Right," he said, and suddenly smiled. The gesture eased an odd boyishness into the normal hardness of his face. "Been a long time since I used the stars as anything but an indication of a fine night. Let's hope the weather holds."

"The forecast is good," Mona said.

"We carry a radio?"

"Receiver and transmitter."

"Fine. Say, why don't you pick off a little sleep?"

"I never felt less sleepy. What or who do you hope to find on Dominica?"

Hood hesitated only momentarily.

"We're looking for a friend," he said quietly.

"And you hope to find him on Dominica?"

"Not necessarily. Maybe somewhere in the Windward Islands."

"Has he run out on his wife or something?"

"He was kidnapped."

The *Goosewing* cleaved on through the gleaming black velvet water.

"Why aren't the police in on this?" Mona asked soberly.

"They were. They could do nothing."

"And you think he is somewhere near Devil's Mountain?"

"Perhaps."

"It sounds dangerous."

"You can always turn back," Hood said casually, looking along the broad path of moonlight.

"You know I won't, damn you."

"Anyhow, soon as you put us ashore you can head for home."

"There is really no danger for you, Miss Gillespie," Murimoto cut in, appearing in the cabin door behind them. "Any trouble will come from ashore. There is no need at all for you to get mixed up in it. For you this should be nothing but a pleasant cruise."

Mona returned his smile, but nothing happened to her eyes. They looked stubborn.

"I might want to get mixed up in it. Maybe I'll hang about and bring this fellow home."

"Oh God," Hood groaned, "a heroine."

"Mark," Murimoto said, a little quickly, "I think you should get some sleep, while the weather is good. I am sure Miss Gillespie can handle things up here, with my inexpert help."

"Of course I can."

"Fine, just fine," said Hood, and couldn't help the jibe in his tone. "With the ship in such capable hands I guess I will get in a little sack time."

"Take all the time you want," she snapped.

"Aye, aye, sir. Call me at four."

Mona glared at his broad back as it slipped through the hatchway leading to the sleeping quarters.

"I wonder why he gets my back up so easily?"

Murimoto wasn't really looking at her, but one part of his sight could notice that the bosom of her bikini was heaving a little more than it should have been. He pursed his lips; it was like a shrug.

At a few minutes to four Hood awoke with the stars paled and the cabin still dark. He was lying on the bunk with his eyes closed and his mind awake when a slim pair of naked legs appeared on the ladder. Hood kept still.

She came up to him. "Mark, it's almost four." There was no reaction. "Like a log," she muttered. "The damn boat could be sinking." She shook him rudely.

His arms wound around her waist and without effort he lifted her onto his nude chest. And held her there tightly.

"Mark! It's me! Mona. Let go of me, damn you!"

It was a creditable effort. Hood groaned, shaking his head and hiding his grin. It was nice having her there along his body; smooth taut belly and smooth long legs. "Oh, it's you. Sorry, I thought I was in trouble."

"You will be if you don't let go of me!"

"Don't fight, Mona. It could be dangerous."

And all the time, in spite of the crude words, he was hoping with male illogic that it wouldn't happen now, so easily; that she would react differently.

Hood was not disappointed. Held there against him, her left hand was still free. It moved swiftly. Only a swifter sideways jerk of his head saved his cheek from four parallel incisions.

He grinned, and let her go.

She shoved herself clear and stood on the deck looking at him with hot eyes. Her bosom threatened to burst free of its inadequate bonds.

"Who do you think you are?" she demanded in a vehement hiss. "What d'you take me for? If you think this is a floating brothel you can jump over the side, right now! You hear me?"

"Loud and clear," said Hood, and swung his legs out. "Blame that damn bikini."

She shook her head slowly and her lips were tight. "Don't you ever try that again."

Hood stood up and reached for his T-shirt. He tried a placating smile. "Mona, I'm sorry," he said simply, and this time he meant it.

"All right," she said, but warily.

"How's the weather?" Hood said matter-of-factly; and he meant that too. This was no pleasure cruise.

CHAPTER

EIGHT

~~~~~~~~~~~~~~~~~~~~~~~~

"Yes, Cuba," Dominat said.

"I see," Tremayne murmured.

They were at breakfast in the huge living room. Outside the morning was bright and hot, but in here it was air-conditionedly cool. The steel shutters were open, with light streaming in through a quartz-textured material, which Tremayne guessed was designed to merge in with the volcano's overall color. A passing pilot might be curious about a square-cut hole in the flank of a mountain.

"I see," Tremayne said again.

It was too fantastic. It was incredible. Tremayne had a strange feeling that he was dreaming. Like Alice, he felt he had stumbled into some crazy improbable world where nothing was real and only the fantastic and grotesque had any meaning.

."Cuba first, then America. We need Cuba as a base from which to launch our attack. It will be almost like the children's game of leapfrog. Cuba; then—as it were—America on the upward bounce."

Tremayne tried to remain calm. It was the only way in which he could maintain a sense of proportion. If he allowed himself to slide into a fever of excitement and panic there would be no way by which he could extricate himself. He had to remain calm. There was a job to be done. He had to stop this madman before he plunged the whole world into complete and utter chaos.

"Yes, the time has come, Tremayne. Our day has come. It has been coming for so long and now it is finally here. In fifteen hours, at midnight, I shall press a button and the first stage of our bid for world conquest will have begun. We are very confident of success."

"Who are 'we'?"

Dominat helped himself to another hot roll. He pulled it apart with his fingers and spread the pieces with butter. Tremayne had noticed that the rolls were fresh.

"I don't mind telling you this because, unfortunately, you will have to die. So, in the best melodramatic tradition I divulge all the details of my evil plot. It is customary, I suppose. But contrary to popular tradition, this time the prisoner will not be rescued in the nick of time. Pity, but the realities of life are so different from popular fiction." Dominat laughed.

"To answer your question, I have gathered together a

band of idealists from the smaller nations of the world. For too long power has been juggled by the so-called 'great' nations, who are rich economically. On their own, these smaller countries have no chance of asserting their rights. But united, and using my ingenious inventions, they can change all that. Do have some more coffee."

Tremayne shook his head. "In other words, you want your own empire."

Dominat refilled his cup. "The ramifications of our organization are so vast that it would be impossible for me to explain them to you in the limited time we have. Suffice it to say, however, that we will change the whole world. America first, then while she is still reeling under the impact of our well-placed crippling blows to her industrial and military complexes, we will loose a series of strikes which will enable us to take over with minimum fuss. By the time everyone has recovered from the shock, our position will have been firmly consolidated. A balance of power will have been restored."

"But why not wait?" Tremayne argued. He knew the argument was feeble, but he continued with it all the same. "These things are being discussed. The world is becoming more enlightened, gradually coming to some form of understanding."

This time Dominat threw his head back when he laughed. "How naive you are, my friend. Are you trying to dissuade me? I hope not, because that would be *too* childish. Our plans have been perfected. The time has come. We are tired of compromise. No more conference tables, no more small-nation politicians crawling on their knees for minor concessions. For the first time they will be able to hold their heads up with pride. Yes. Power. That is the only answer."

The man was a fanatic. As he spoke, Tremayne could see the gleam in his eyes and hear the vibrant breathlessness in his voice. He wanted the power for himself, of course. All this talk about giving small nations their rights might fool them, but Tremayne had seen it all before.

". . . so much to answer for," he was saying. "How I have lived for this moment, how many times I have told myself that one day the world would be changed through my scientific achievements. So I studied, Mr. Tremayne, I worked until my head reeled, night and day, and then, as more people came to join me and pour money into my coffers, I knew that I would succeed. Many, many idealists came to offer their services. Oh yes."

Tremayne's sense of unreality was deepening. He had to snap himself out of it. "Dominat," he said, "you are mad."

His intention was as deliberate as his tone was casual. The giant was letting him live for only one purpose —to boast. Dominat was trying to justify his actions, particularly to Tremayne, the cultured Englishman, to whom, however unconsciously, he felt inferior. Tremayne decided to adopt a contemptuous attitude. This was his only hold over Dominat, and on life. Once Dominat thought he had proved himself superior, then the game was done with.

Right now Tremayne thought that that limit might have been reached. Dominat's face tightened and his eyes were cold. But then he veiled his eyes and forced a smile.

"I am beginning to wonder," he murmured, reaching for the marmalade, "just how much longer I can put up with your insolence."

"Or with my knowledge of your insecurity?" Tremayne inquired. "You sent me that girl last night. You don't really give a damn whether I slept with her or not. What worries you is the fact that I rejected your offer. To your mind that sort of thing corresponds to the rejection of an order. And that you cannot tolerate. You know why? Because, surrounded by your gimmickry and frightened lackeys, you are still unsure of yourself. I'm afraid, old cnap, that you are not really leadership material."

Two patches of white burned at the corners of

Dominat's mouth, but he had command of himself. He stood up.

"Finish your breakfast. I have some business to attend to. I will join you shortly and then I shall *show* you some of the reaches of my power."

The main door closed behind him. Tremayne looked at the breakfast table. It was laid lavishly, with the same sort of extravagance that had furnished the room. From the selection of kidneys, chops, sausages, and steak, each in its heated dish on the sideboard, he had selected fresh eggs and ham; it had been delicious. Now there awaited him enough toast for a platoon, and bananas, mangoes, avocadoes, guavas, oranges, grapefruit.

Tremayne poured himself another cup of coffee.

He took his cup to the great window and looked out. The view was tinted, but otherwise perfectly clear. He knocked a knuckle against the 'glass.' It sounded solid. He searched for a button or switch but found only the one that had opened the steel shutters.

Tremayne looked down the smooth glinting lava slope and over the forest and the seagirt village far below and he wondered, with a sense of hopelessness that almost swamped him, where the hell was Hood? The big fellow would hang on like a bulldog.

If he could. Dominat had indicated that he intended to have Hood killed, but if he had succeeded, he would surely have boasted about it to Tremayne.

And while Hood was still alive there was hope. Almost certainly the police would have learned that Borja's house was burned, but that was no help. No friend could have sighted the seaplane, nobody knew where he was. He was trapped in this macabre nightmare of a fortress with no hope of rescue; at the mercy of an egomaniacal genius who would keep him alive just long enough to prove his superiority.

Tremayne turned from the window and saw that the giant had returned and was watching him, smiling. Dominat was wearing an open-necked shirt and shorts with sandals. Tremayne thought he had never seen so perfect a specimen of musculature, and certainly not a bigger one. The fellow exuded a dominating oppressiveness.

"Admiring the view?" Dominat said.

Tremayne was careful to match his smile; to some degree Dominat had to be mad, and he must not be allowed to see that his guest was fearful or impressed.

"Remotely, you might say," Tremayne answered. He walked back to the table and replaced his cup. "A man could become bored, incarcerated here for any length of time."

"I will show you something to stimulate your interest."

"Your vanity, perhaps. I have no interest in your mechanical toys."

Dominat studied him a moment with his head on one side. "You are a fool to try and appear so uninterested," he said mildly. "You are obviously an agent. You are also human, and therefore you must have some hope of getting away from here. And certainly you wish to take with you as much knowledge as you possibly can. So why not drop this pose of languid boredom?"

"Wrong again," Tremayne lied; the more boredom he showed, the more, he hoped, he would be shown of this fantastic place. "Being an agent, as you say I am, I'm a fatalist. A wiser man than I opined that all things must come to an end. I've reached mine. There is no chance whatever of my getting away from here. I know it, you know it. So why pretend interest in things I can't tell about? However, if you insist on this Cook's tour I suppose I must play along."

Dominat frowned slightly. "I am not quite sure about you, Tremayne. Whether you are specious, honest, clever, or all three."

Tremayne shrugged.

"Come on," Dominat said abruptly. "And be careful," he warned over his shoulder, "to touch nothing. Do exactly as you are told, otherwise the end you mentioned is likely to come sooner than you think. You will see strange and dangerous things. Follow me." They left the room.

All compartments seemed to open from the central core of the elevator shaft. They entered a room which was strictly utilitarian. The floor was concrete but the walls and domed ceiling were living rock. The room held nothing but a small console of dials and switches, two men in white coats, and a black rectangular box about three feet long which rested on a block of solid, smoothly hewn granite.

"This," Dominat said, flicking a finger at the black box, "is the prototype of my entire power supply. The power station is sited in the base of the mountain. Steam turbines, of course. The big brother of this one provides the steam—at five hundred pounds per square inch working pressure, which is really quite enormous; greater, in fact, that that produced in the boiler room of a battleship in World War Two. And I do it all," he said proudly, "with wires."

"Which is nonsense, of course."

"Of course. Stand away from the door."

Tremayne obeyed; after what he'd seen so far he would believe anything of this weird ménage in the bowels of a mountain. Dominat walked to the console at the front of the box and flicked a switch. In the side of the black box facing the door a small panel slid open. From his position Tremayne could see nothing, but involuntarily he stepped back farther.

Dominat came forward. He took out a handkerchief. Carefully, holding his arm well out from his body, he lowered the handkerchief in front of the opened panel, but at least three yards from it. Tremayne saw the bottom edge of the cloth begin to curl. Dominat dropped it. For a second the handkerchief seemed to hang suspended by some invisible force; it curled and twisted, and then it dropped to the floor, and the astonished Tremayne saw that now it was nothing but a tiny heap of charred carbon.

"That," said Dominat, "is heat."

The Englishman tried to be casual. "That," he said,

nodding at the box, "is nothing but an electric furnace, with the heat concentrated into a beam."

Dominat smiled. "A good, if uneducated, guess." He shut the panel, but already Tremayne noticed how hot the room had become. "Perhaps as a boy, you tried to break a wire by twisting it? You will remember that before it broke, the wire became quite hot around the point where it was being twisted?" Tremayne nodded. "The same principle is applied in this box, and in the larger working model. A much more sophisticated arrangement, of course, but the basic precepts are similar."

"You mean wires are just being twisted in there? Really!"

"They are not ordinary wires, my friend, and they are not being just twisted. Let me try to explain. No doubt you know that the flow of electricity through a conductor can be likened to the flow of water through a hose? But here no electricity is used, not, at least, as you know it. Through my wires a stream of electrons is forced at extremely high pressure, like water through a hose. What happens when a hose under pressure is dropped? It snakes and curls all over the place. Twists, in other words. But to generate heat a wire has to be twisted much more violently than a snaking hose. And here"—Dominat smiled—"enters genius. I have devised a method of enormously amplifying, that is to say increasing, the electron flow. I call my method 'fluidic control.' The specially treated wires in this box oscillate at incredible speed. But see for yourself."

Tremayne hesitated, then he remembered that Dominat could finish him in a much less macabre manner than this if he wanted to. He walked over and stood beside the giant at the rear of the black box. Dominat lifted a metallic cover in its top.

"Look."

Tremayne leaned forward and peered down. There was a window of the same clear quartz material as that filling the opening in Dominat's room. Through it he could see what looked like thousands of slender wires, as though the core of a big telephone cable had been bared of its insulation.

"Come back," Dominat ordered. "Put these on."

He handed Tremayne a pair of welder's glasses. The agent put them on.

"And now," Dominat said triumphantly, as he flicked the switch again, "look again!"

Tremayne edged forward. The rectangle of quartz was glowing. He looked in, then, as he focused, his eyes widened in astonishment. A white glare beat against his goggles. Through their heavily tinted lenses he saw that the quiescent wires were now oscillating galvanically like a mass of demented worms. Yet the most impressive thing about this extraordinary box was the fact that he felt no heat, though his eyes told him that inside it was a white-hot furnace.

Dominat switched off. At once the glare died, the worms were quiet again. Tremayne handed back the goggles.

"Interesting," he murmured.

"Not incredible, fantastic? Or even clever?"

All of these things, Tremayne thought, remembering the handkerchief; not even the opened door of a battle-ship's furnace could have produced that result.

"I really can't judge, can I? One supposes that the very first furnace caused wonder in the eyes of the beholders. These days a child wouldn't be impressed by it. For all I know this device of yours might be in common use in American industry."

"No," said Dominat slowly, "you can't be that stupid." Yet he looked disappointed, almost petulant, and Tremayne knew that he'd gained for himself at least a few more hours of life. "Follow me," Dominat said curtly.

Tremayne turned slowly, and the instinct of training, if not hope, had his eyes running over the console and fil- ing in his memory the switches he'd seen Dominat use. But this was purely reactive, and he could imagine no possible way in which he could use his knowledge to advantage.

They stepped into the elevator.

"Down here," Dominat said after several seconds of descent, when Tremayne judged they must be near the mountain's base, "I am extending my house, shall we say."

Their swift fall came to a smooth stop. The door opened and Tremayne stepped out behind his guide and grinding thunder beat against his eardrums. He pressed his hands to his head. Dominat reached up to hooks on the wall and handed him a pair of large-muffed earphones and a tiny throat mike. Putting them on, Tremayne was grateful for the instant easing of that cavernous sound. Then he heard Dominat's voice.

"You are served by an inbuilt transistor radio. To speak, just press the microphone against your larynx. Follow me."

Tremayne obeyed. Here there was no splendor, vulgar or otherwise; he was walking through a rock tunnel which just accommodated his height—Dominat had to stoop. Tremayne was intrigued by the sides and roof of the tunnel where the rock was quite smooth, almost as if it had been concreted.

"You will notice the lighting is of unusual brilliance," said Dominat from a few paces ahead of him. Tremayne had been thinking of the unworrying contempt inherent in this relative position of the big man; plainly Dominat expected no foolish actions from his guest. "This is because the filaments are burning in iodine gas, another of my designs. Here we are. On no account," warned Dominat, "remove your earphones. If you do your eardrums will be ruptured."

Tremayne believed him. Involuntarily he settled the muffs more securely about his ears. Even so he could hear a dull rumble like distant gunfire as he stepped into a huge cavern.

"This will be the assembly hangar for my missiles," he heard.

Tremayne looked about him wonderingly. On the far side in front of him the domed wall of the cavern was holed like a Swiss cheese; there seemed to be a succession of tunnels about three feet in diameter and spaced the same distance apart. And to the right of the right-hand opening a thick stream of some material spewed backward into the cavern. But from above this strange ejection water sprayed onto it, and the air remained free of dust.

"You see?" Dominat said, pointing at the holes. "Divide and conquer."

"No, I don't see."

"You will. Follow me closer."

Dominat stopped. "Now perhaps you can see how I divide and conquer this tough old Mountain of the Devil."

"No," said Tremayne truthfully.

"Look at those tunnels, man! They have been bored into the rock as an auger bites into wood. Very soon I will be ready to bore transverse tunnels across their axis. Then that solid rock will be honeycombed, and then small packages of plastic explosive will collapse it, and my hangar will have its radius extended by another fifty feet."

"In how many years?" Tremayne sneered, and knew his sneer was the defensive reaction to the frightened wonder which filled him at this madman's power to genius.

Dominat laughed. "To be precise, in one day, perhaps a trifle longer. My atoborer could do it in a matter of minutes, but there is no pressing urgency."

"Atoborer?" said Tremayne, weakly.

"This." Dominat gave an order to the group of workmen standing nearby and the ejected stream of chewed rock ceased. Another order. One of the workmen moved a lever on a portable console.

"Radio control," Dominat said. "You may remove your earphones now."

Tremayne had them half off when a monstrous thing that looked like a giant artillery shell three feet thick came backing out of the new tunnel. It moved with a regular clanking on caterpillar treads, and now Tremayne could see that instead of a shell's smooth conical nose this thing wore a great corkscrew on its sloping shoulders.

"My little gimlet." Dominat smiled at his bewilderment. "It is self-propelled, and powered by a small atomic reactor of immense capacity. The threaded nose revolves, of course, and bites into that rock like an auger into cheese." He stepped up beside the still-backing borer, and lifting a countersunk panel, he thumbed a button. The clanking ceased, the thing stopped. It stood there on its treads, the rock-dusted nose seeming to sniff at the hole it had made; an ugly metallic mole.

"One press to stop, another to go," Dominat explained. "One must provide an auxiliary control in case of radio malfunction. Now, my friend, what do you think of this little tool?"

Tremayne slowly shook his head. "It bored out all this?"

"The whole complex, every single compartment. And of course the elevator shaft. But one must be careful," Dominat went on in a lecturing tone, yet his eyes were glinting with pleasure at the expression on Tremayne's face. "One must keep a tight rein on her, otherwise she would bore right through to the crater, and then she would drop into God knows what below."

"But the volcano's extinct!"

"Is a volcano ever extinct? Was Vesuvius when it buried Pompeii, or Krakatoa when it split an island in half?" Dominat chuckled. "But we need not worry. Our Mountain of the Devil has done his dash, at least for the foreseeable future. I had a volcanologist examine my piece of real estate before I started to build."

"What happened to the volcanologist?" Tremayne asked grimly.

Dominat shrugged. "He was a curious as well as a studious fellow. Too curious. One day he happened to slip from the edge of the crater. Perhaps he wanted to see what lay at its bottom. He found out."

"But not before his report was made."

"Yes, we were fortunate to have his report in time. Speaking of time . . ." Dominat glanced at his watch. "There is just time. Come quickly."

As the elevator door slid closed it shut out the beginning of that grinding thunder Tremayne had first heard, and he knew Dominat's atoborer was again at its disemboweling work. What a device for commercial mining, he thought, and then the elevator stopped and he found himself on a steel platform. Waiting there, resting on a monorail, was a streamlined machine about twelve feet long. It was sheathed with gleaming aluminum and looked like a rocket. Especially the ramjet tail.

"This will take us down to the village," Dominat explained, gesturing Tremayne to step inside.

Tremayne was a competent mechanical engineer. Despite the hatred and disgust he felt for this devil beside him, he had to know.

"What speed are we doing?" he shouted.

"About three hundred knots. I could better that, but the distance is so short. In fact . . ." Dominat leaned forward to a lever and retro-rockets thrust out a fiercely denying hand. "We are already there."

They disembarked. They were in the open, with the village only a few yards down the hardtop road. It was a ramshackle cluster of huts, with palms and almond trees lining the beach side of the main street.

Dominat carried no visible weapon but Tremayne knew with harsh certitude that even if he could escape those great hands and reach the jungle, the giant would send his men swarming after him. Tremayne tried to cover his despair with nonchalance. He was surprised to see that, instead of the dirt tracks to be expected in a place so primitive, the main street was smoothly coated with bitumen.

"Where to now?"

"Down to the harbor." Dominat began striding, so that Tremayne had to walk quickly to keep up. "What you will see is only a minor tool, understand, but it is useful."

"A submarine?"

"No, not exactly. You will see."

They halted on the pier. On the way down Tremayne's

attention had been as much for the villagers as for Dominat's fantastic story—and his hope was stillborn. They did not actually bow or knuckle forelocks, but their attitude of deference was the same. Whether through loyalty or respect or plain fear, Dominat was patently supreme here.

"What do you think of her? See, she enters. She floats!"

The thing was more like a beetle, without guns but with treads that obviously were acting also as propelling paddles. Yet it was as big as a Tiger tank, and seemed to be doing about thirty knots.

"It's submerging now," the inventor gloated.

"True enough," Tremayne muttered, more to himself. "But will it surface?"

Dominat looked at him pityingly. "This morning has taught you nothing of my skills? Borja, a man preeminent in his field, thinks me a genius."

"Borja thought," Tremayne corrected.

The calm water of the harbor broke and a humpbacked shape shouldered through. The tank turned handily. A hatch opened and a scuba-suited figure appeared. It waved.

Dominat waved back in a "carry on" gesture. The hatch closed and the tank turned for the mouth of the bay.

"It's going out to sea?" Tremayne asked.

"Right out. Through Dominica Passage to the north and then one hundred miles due west. We have a number of machines positioned just out of radar range off the principal Cuban ports. Their main function is to sabotage the naval installations. While traveling, it will surface at dawn and sunset, but purely for navigational purposes, to take star and sun sights."

But Tremayne had lost interest in the tank, now turning to head north. "When do I get to see your missiles?"

Dominat hesitated, then he smiled. His eyes did not. "You are unwise to be so eager, my friend. Once you see that, there is nothing left for you to see. And I quite enjoy talking to a man like you." He glanced at his watch, while Tremayne felt cold in the day's heat. "We shall lunch now. Come."

There was a small cabin cruiser anchored no more than a hundred yards out in the bay. Tremayne's eyes fastened on it as he measured his chances. Perhaps it carried a radio. The plan was born of hopelessness and acted upon instantly through the compulsion of desperation. Dominat's back was to him. Tremayne tugged off his shoes, ran to the end of the pier, and dived into the water.

A voice shouted. Dominat wheeled. He turned back leisurely and spoke one word. Three Caribs raced into the water from the beach. They had been born to the water. They overtook Tremayne before he had gone fifty yards. They hauled him inshore and dumped him at Dominat's feet on the sand. Dominat bent. He took Tremayne's arm and lifted him with one hand. He placed the other hand, opened, across the Englishman's belly and tossed him like a doll fifteen feet along the beach.

Tremayne was exhausted by his fight in the water but he had sense enough to tuck his head in and land rolled up in a ball. He hit the sand with a *whoof* of exploded breath. He got to his knees, panting.

"Come here," said Dominat quietly.

"Come and get me, damn you," Tremayne grated, and stood groggily on his feet in a boxing stance.

Dominat gestured. The three Caribs took him. Two held his arms while the third clubbed him into unconsciousness. Dominat gestured again. They took Tremayne to the gleaming rocket device on the monorail. Smiling faintly, Dominat looked after them.

Then he looked out to sea. But the amphibious tank had vanished beyond the point.

CHAPTER

NINE

~~~~~~~~~~~~~~~~~~~~

"I MAKE IT about a hundred and thirty miles to go," said Hood. "That's a good three hours at this speed."

It was about three o'clock on a sultry afternoon. They were in the cabin, standing side by side, with the chart on the table. The boat, catching the side of a wave, lurched. Mona had just put her hands to her hair. She stumbled. Hood was quick. One big arm went out and held her tightly. For a moment Mona stayed there, her body tensed and quiet and her eyes on the chart. Then Hood felt her body slacken. He eased his hold. She turned within the compass of his arm and looked directly into his eyes. Hood swallowed. This was one of those electrically-charged moments. Her mouth came forward.

"All right," she said, so low he barely heard. "Be quick."

Ten minutes later Murimoto called, "Below there. Squall coming down from the north."

They climbed back into the cabin. Mona stared to port. She said, crisply decisive:

"Head her up into it."

Not all of Hood's thoughts were of seamanship as he went forward. Women were supposed to be docile and melting after they'd been mastered. Not this one. Like hell. Seemed she'd just used him, like a release valve. He grinned. So he was a valve.

The black line came slewing across the sea and reached them. The sea boiled like milk. *Goosewing* was clubbed over. Rain that sounded like lead pellets rattled against the hull. Mona was at the wheel and the boat creamed and hissed through the sea. A few minutes of violence and she had thrust again into clear water, with the squall cat's-pawing its way to the southward.

"My God!" Mona ejaculated. "What on earth's that?"

Hood's reaction was swift, and based on old training in another field. An exclamation like that on a bridge meant trouble, and trouble you had to see clearly. He bent down and grabbed his binoculars from a seat locker. They were already focused, so that he saw the thing immediately, a half-mile ahead of the bow.

"A monster," decided Murimoto, from a training steeped in legend.

"The whale."

"If that's a whale," Hood said from under his binoculars, "it's complete with Jonah—sticking his head up through a hatch in the backbone."

"Good Lord!" Mona spun the wheel.

"Maintain your heading," Hood commanded.

"Why?"

"Because it's submerging. I don't know what it is, but don't let them think they've been sighted."

"Let me have the glasses."

Hood held on to them. "Small spouts of water—that means ballast tanks blowing. Yes, I've seen it before." He turned to Murimoto. "At the Serrana Bank."

"Then it *is* a submarine," Mona breathed.

"A submarine makes hardly any bow wave as it dives. That thing seems to be thrashing under, like it had paddles or something. Now it's gone. Steady as you go. We'll pass over the submerging point."

Mona did not demur at the authority in his tone. She said, "Could there be any danger, Mark?"

"I doubt it. Not as long as we act normally. Murimoto, take over the wheel. Mona, come out here and sit down." Hood sat down on a bench. "We're just out on a pleasure cruise. Look as if you're enjoying it. That thing might have a periscope."

The *Goosewing* pressed steadily on with its crew apparently unconcerned. Until Mona said, "Something's shining on the water ahead," and Hood raised his glasses.

But first he made a wide search, quartering carefully the sea ahead and on either bow. He saw nothing, no reflecting periscopic eye or feathery wake. Then he lowered his sight and quite plainly he saw the spreading slick of pretty iridescence.

"Oil," he grunted. "Don't heave to. I'm thinking we weren't meant to see your whale, and we wouldn't have if we hadn't come bursting out of that rain squall."

Suddenly Mona froze, and then she whispered, "Oh no! Look!"

Hood's head swung. His eyes squinted in wonderment. The thing was right there alongside, a smooth metallic beetly thing that kept pace with them not more than fifteen yards out. It had come around behind them. He heard a faint whining sound, and recognized it as electric motors, and then with a sharp clang a circular hatch was flung open and a man's upper body appeared. Hood saw the barrel of a submachine gun pointed at his guts.

Mona did not speak. She could not. With his hand below deck level, Hood gestured behind him to Murimoto in the cabin.

"Play it cool," he warned. "Nice and easy." He raised his voice. "Who are you? What do you want?"

The gun barrel lifted a little. "We sink your boat. You come with us."

"But why, for God's sake?" Hood made his voice concerned.

"You saw us," he was informed simply. "Stop your boat."

The engines died.

"Now look here. We've done nothing. You can't do this to us!"

The barrel edged forward. "You come, or die here."

Hood combed his fingers through his hair. "I don't understand. . . . Where are you taking us?"

The gunman hesitated, then his teeth showed whitely. "To Morne au Diable. You will see. Now stop the boat, quick."

"All right, all right! For God's sake, don't fire." Hood turned his head and spoke out of the corner of his mouth. "No false moves," he grunted. "Act scared."

"I don't have to act," Mona whispered back. "Can't we do something?"

"Wait for the order. Both of you. Murimoto, in a minute, move out of the cabin door with your hands in the air. Look scared." Murimoto nodded.

Mona said, "You're going to let those swine take my boat? You've got a gun!"

"It's below."

The lower half of his body was concealed from the eyes of the watcher on the strange craft. He kicked open a bench locker, still looking across at their captor. He waited until the man's attention was suddenly distracted by the appearance of Murimoto in the doorway, then his hands dived into the locker. It took only a split second. He straightened. The man with the gun had apparently noticed nothing. In his hands Hood was holding two grenades he had had the foresight to bring with him.

"Good," said the man in the hatch. "You are wise. Now we come close, then you come on board. You do not go below in your boat."

He lowered his head to speak down the hatch and at once a small white thrashing started along the sides of the weird craft. It headed in toward them.

Hood waited until the submersible was almost alongside. The commander lowered his head again, presumably to give an order. Hood raised his right arm.

The light was failing and a man's face makes a small target. But this thrower had for years made the tops of three cricket stumps his target. He flung out his right arm until it extended straight behind his head, the left arm balancing in front of him. For a second he was still, and then he threw.

Its pin still in, the grenade shot across the gap like a bullet. The gunman's head came up as the craft's nose began its leveling turn. Its steel skin fashioned like a pineapple's, ugly and hard and forceful, the grenade smashed into his forehead. So fiercely that his body was jerked backward and hung down halfway out of the hatch.

"Down!" Hood roared. "Flat on the deck!"

Then he leaned over as far as he could and gently, with precision, he tossed his unpinned second grenade down through the hatch.

There was no real danger, not on the outside. Even the explosion sounded as a small *crump*. But inside dozens of raised steel rectangles were blown into jagged slivers that screamed around the control room and burst into men's bodies.

Hood jumped up from the deck. Knowing that a grenade could have caused no vital structural damage, he guessed that the craft was nosing under because some shocked hand had pushed a wrong lever. But right then he was not much interested in causes, only in fact. And the fact was swift inexorable death, for already water was lapping in over the hatch coaming and then cascading, pouring down in a resistless, flooding column three feet thick as the craft swam under the surface. There came a nasty gurgling sound, as of bath water running away, but harshly magnified, then big bubbles rose and burst quietly on the empty surface. Something shimmered faintly down in the depths, and was lost. Hood turned away.

"Come on, let's go," he ordered.

CHAPTER

TEN

~~~~~~

"YOU ARE not eating." Dominat smiled as he looked at Tremayne across the lunch table. "Our little game on the beach bruised your ribs, perhaps?" He pursed his lips admonishingly. "That was a foolish attempt, quite without hope. A word, you know, and they would have drowned you like a kitten." Dominat took an orange and started peeling it thoughtfully. "You are very fortunate that I am able to devote so much time to you. But everything is ready now, and all we have to do is wait. I have a number of important guests staying with me at the moment. Regional leaders of my organization. By rights I should be entertaining them, but frankly, I rather enjoy your company."

"I wish I could say the same."

The colossus gave a grunting belch of laughter. Both hands slapped his drum of a chest. "Yes, you amuse me. You can't deny now that what you've seen here impresses you, can you, Tremayne?"

For the past few hours Tremayne had thought long and hard about what he might gain. He sensed that Dominat was growing tired of the novelty of his presence. In formulating his plan he had nothing to lose but a life that he believed forfeit anyhow. Yet if he won, and Dominat died, there was just the faintest edge of a chance that he might escape, after sabotaging the first phase of the madman's operation—Sugarstrike. He took a deep breath.

"I think you are a coward," he said, using all the contempt he could muster.

"Are you throwing down the gauntlet?"

"Yes, I am."

Dominat laughed. "You are a fool."

"A gun," said Tremayne. "A gun makes a man ten feet tall."

"Quite so. But I would not fight a midget if he had a gun." Dominat chuckled. "Providing he kept his distance, that is."

"And if you and I both had guns?"

"What?"

"I see that changes matters," Tremayne needled him. "That would make us equal. You don't fancy those odds?" He spooned sugar into his coffee and smiled as he stirred. "Actually I can't blame you. I have some skill with a pistol."

"Do I understand you are proposing a duel?"

Tremayne's heart jumped but he kept his face composed; Dominat was not smiling now and his face was intent.

"That's right, a duel." The twist of Tremayne's mouth made his smile a shrug. "But I propose, and Dominat disposeth. Rightly, of course. Why should you accept such a challenge?"

"I know you are baiting me."

"So wisely, you refuse to take the bait. Like a fox, or a rat, Dominat. Not like a lion."

Dominat smiled again, yet without pleasure, Tremayne thought.

"Perhaps I don't enjoy your company so much, after all. Why should I give you the chance of killing me?"

"So you admit there is a chance you might lose? Against men with no chance you are a veritable Samson, a Goliath. But when the odds are even slightly shaded, why then . . ."

Tremayne let his voice fade off to silence. He noticed Dominat's great fingers were spread on the table. He took up his coffee cup in a gesture that managed to convey he thought the argument was over, and won.

"I repeat," Dominat said harshly, "you are a fool."

Tremayne nodded. "I'm everything you like to call me. Except one thing." He lowered his cup. It met the saucer with a small definite sound that seemed loud in the silent room. "Dominat," he said, very quietly, "I may die here; I expect to. Normally to a man like you the death of another man means no more than the tossing out of that orange. But after I die, you will always remember that there was one English gentleman who believed you to be basically a coward."

White spots were burning at the corners of Dominat's mouth as he slowly stood up. For a moment he looked malevolently down at Tremayne, and then he strode to the aluminum desk. Tremayne turned in his chair to watch him. Dominat pressed a button. The end door opened. Mero slouched in. From a drawer Dominat took three pistols. He handed one to Mero.

"Check it."

Mero broke the barrel. He inspected the chambers, looked through the barrel, snapped the thing together again, then drew back and released the hammer. Dumbly, he nodded up to the big man.

"Tremayne and I will stand back to back," Dominat said. "When I order 'Now' we will each march ten paces away from each other. I will go toward the window, he will go toward the door. At the end of ten paces we will turn and fire. If he turns before then, if he tries in any way to cheat, you will shoot him through the head. You understand?"

Mero grinned his understanding. He held the gun negligently, in the manner of a man who knew how to use it. Tremayne got up and walked to the desk.

"There was really no need for all that," he said pleasantly. "I trust you to walk the full ten paces—or is that being foolish?"

Dominat did not answer him, though his eyes were dark and agate-hard. He handed Tremayne a pistol. Tremayne broke it.

"Nice odds," he murmured. "It's not loaded."

"It will be. Come."

They walked to the center of the huge room and stood back to back. While Dominat handed his opponent six shells and Tremayne loaded the chambers, Mero watched him with pale unblinking eyes. Tremayne finished and drew back the hammer. There was a chance here—one into Mero's belly, then a whirl and the muzzle against Dominat's back—but Tremayne thought the odds too uneven.

Though his muscles were taut his mind was calm. Tremayne was an expert pistol shot; more importantly here, perhaps, he was a quick shot, for these things he had trained himself to be, assiduously; he had none of Hood's karate skill. He did not doubt that he could hit Dominat's great chest. Then he would swivel to the right and kill Mero, and then it would be the giant's turn again, if the first bullet had not completed its job.

Standing there, Tremayne felt the first surge, not of relief or hope, but of triumph. Deliberately he killed that mind-disturbing sensation, and quietly he waited. The room was totally silent.

"Now," said Dominat.

They separated. Tremayne walked, he did not stride, for his body must not be unbalanced at the end of this pregnant progress. He counted, the gun hand held level with his hip, the elbow pressed in, ready for the whirl. Seven . . . eight . . . nine . . . The tenth pace brought his right foot to the ground and Tremayne swiveled fast on the ball of it as his trigger finger took up the first pressure. He saw Dominat's bulk and knew he had marched the full ten paces. Then his finger was squeezing finally, but a fraction of a split second before the hammer was released there jolted against his hand a numbing shock and the pistol flew backward as if tugged by a wire.

The sound of Dominat's shot crashed around the room. Tremayne stood before him helpless. He wanted to close his eyes. He kept them open, staring at the small black hole which looked malignantly back into his face. Dominat lowered his gun.

He was smiling again. "Now?" he said, softly.

Life, even if circumscribed, is sweet. Tremayne breathed in slowly. Regardless of the differences in their characters, they had faced the barrier, these two. This was a time for honesty.

"Yes," said Tremayne. "You're a damn good pistol shot."

"Thank you." Dominat collected the guns, unloaded and stowed them away, then gestured Mero out. The door closed silently. "And you, my desperate friend, are still a fool."

"Why didn't you finish it?" Tremayne murmured.

Dominat chuckled. "Because I haven't finished showing you my domain."

"Yes, of course."

Tremayne obeyed with dull resignation. This time it seemed the elevator dropped him even lower than the level where the atoborer was at work. They stepped out into the same type of drilled, beautifully smooth tunnel —yet this one seemed at least three times wider than normal, and running into it Tremayne saw a set of railroad tracks.

As they walked Tremayne noticed something else. The sight surprised him, even though it shouldn't have, for he was looking simply at sunlight; but this was the first time he had seen natural light inside the mountain.

"We're heading for the crater?"

"Not the crater, but another example of my atoborer's skill. You will see."

A minute later Tremayne saw. "Good Lord," he mumbled.

Then he resumed his study of what lay before him, brightly lit by the morning sun. He had no great knowledge of rocketry but he could appreciate form, and his engineering mind gave this device full marks—it was a long, upright, shining needle of a thing about fifty feet high; a greyhound among rockets, he thought. No great moon-seeking bullock of a rocket, but something that looked as if it could leap in a flash from its pad straight into fantastic speed.

He looked at the pad. The rocket was standing on a solid metallic circle, but this base was not on rock—it was suspended, level with him and halfway down the aperture that had been drilled through the sloping side of the mountain, by a gleaming spider web of slender beams that had their peripheral ends embedded in the solid rock. Those strands were not of steel; they seemed fragile to suspend such a central weight, but Tremayne guessed they must be of immense tensile strength. He noted a group of men working around the rocket's base.

"Sugarstrike," Dominat said. "It is ready to be fired."

CHAPTER

ELEVEN

~~~~~~~~~~~~~~~~~~~~

"THERE'S THE Mountain of the Devil," said Hood. "You can't argue with the chart."

"So it's a mountain. There's nothing else here—no village or towns, not even a bay we can sail into, nothing but cliffs."

"There must be a way in," Hood said, but there was

a lightness in his tone that made her look at him, and then quickly turn to follow the direction of his finger. "There's your village, and your bay."

"You think your friend's in there?" Mona asked.

"I mean to find out."

"Radio?" Murimoto suggested.

"No profit in tipping our hand. At the first squawk for help they'd have him out of there in nothing flat. Okay, we're going in."

Goosewing curved around the cliffy shoulder. As he headed her in Hood studied the anchorage. He saw the cabin cruiser, moored to a buoy, then appraised the pier. It was quite long and looked solidly built for a place so small and isolated.

They anchored a short distance from the other boat and went in the rest of the way in the dinghy, across water shadowed by the volcano's bulk against the lowering sun. Murimoto had no gun, but Hood's .38 rested comfortingly next to his spine under the jacket. He was worried about Mona's presence, yet she could not be left alone on board, and he had not bargained for this possibly direct contact with the man he was after. So she was here, and there was nothing he could do about it.

"A welcoming committee," Hood said.

But when he ran the dinghy in against the pier steps and they climbed up, the group of Caribs made no attempt to molest or even question them. They simply stared at them. Hood picked one at random.

"What's the name of this place?"

"Dominat."

"Dominat? It's not marked . . ." Hood started, but the Carib turned and walked quickly along the pier.

"Oh well," Hood said, "sun's well over the yardarm. Come on." They started walking. The group followed. Hood took Mona's arm. "Don't worry, honey," he said softly. "If I can't look after you Murimoto surely will."

Mona did not answer.

As they reached the end of the pier another group

of men was waiting for them. "Oh—oh," Hood muttered. "Trouble."

The men held guns. They were surrounded.

"You didn't take long to get here," a deep voice said behind them.

Many men have deep voices, even some small men. Yet for no reason that he could pin down Hood felt a cold feathering of antagonism and caution up and down his spine. He turned slowly, and as he turned he flicked open the button of his jacket.

The man who faced them, his eyes squinting into the westering sun, was a giant.

"You were expecting us?" Hood asked conversationally.

"Of course. Thank you, Mona. You have done a good job."

Mona stepped forward and stood beside the giant. "It was too easy," she said.

"Of course," Hood said slowly. "First you tried to kill me, then when you didn't succeed, you decided to lure us here."

"Something like that," Mona replied. "I radioed ahead while I was waiting for you on the boat at Kingston."

"And I sent a craft to intercept you," Dominat said. "What has happened to it?"

Mona told him.

"Well, Mr. Hood, you have done me a great disservice. I don't like that. Mona had been instructed to get you here without any trouble. The killing attempts were, I admit, clumsy. In many fields I am served by amateurs. By bringing you here I shall now be able to dispose of you to my own satisfaction."

"And Mona?" Hood asked.

Dominat's arm was around Mona's waist. "Mona has many uses. She is an exciting woman. She is also an idealist. I have many idealists working for me. They are useful allies. Oh, by the way, your Mr. Tremayne is here too. I shall take you to him."

Dominat turned to Murimoto. "Who is this?"

"His name's Murimoto," said Hood. "He is my servant."

"Japanese? I do not like Japanese." With the last word Dominat's hand struck. It went open, with contempt, and its palm took Murimoto, the man who could avoid a flung bottle, across his face. Murimoto uttered a gasp of pain and stumbled backward.

Dominat chuckled.

Hood took a step forward. "You're a good hand here, surrounded by all your own men. If we were alone . . ."

"Don't waste your breath, Hood," Dominat sneered. "Search them."

Murimoto's clothes revealed nothing dangerous, but on Hood they found the .38. He was secretly surprised, for though he'd been thoroughly searched before—between the thighs, under the armpits and even inside his socks—this was only the second time anyone had discovered the lumbar holster.

With no threatening gesture or tone, yet with complete surety in his casualness, Dominat said, "Follow me."

With his arm around Mona he led the way up the hardtop road. The two captives followed him, and a quiet watchful group of Caribs brought up the rear.

Hood was silent. There was nothing to say to Murimoto; one didn't advise a man like Murimoto as to when to make the move. They climbed to the platform and were whisked into the mountain, then up in the elevator. Dominat also was silent, but obviously he was enjoying the astonishment Hood's face expressed. Murimoto's face remained as composedly enigmatic as a Buddha's. Then they were in the sybaritic living room, and at last Dominat spoke.

"We are in the belly of the Mountain of the Devil—something your chart did not show, I imagine?" His hand waved. "I was in the middle of some interesting entertainment when your arrival interrupted it. But presently it shall be continued." He coughed. "I believe you two have already met?"

First off, on entering the huge room, Hood's eyes had

swept it in a trained encompassing study; he ignored the furnishings and noted there were two doors, both now closed, and one odd-looking window. And that four big Caribs had followed them in. All of them carried knives.

This initial examination was practiced and self-preservative. Now, at Dominat's last words, he looked at the other human element in the room.

"Tommy. Thank God."

Tremayne advanced across the room. "Mark, not you, too?" His voice was doleful. "He'll kill us both, you know."

Hood turned back to Dominat. "What *will* you do to us?"

While Hood was speaking and Dominat's attention was momentarily diverted, Tremayne did a strange thing—at least, it seemed strange to Hood. He was well clear of all of them, but instead of trying to get closer to his friends he went in a stumbling rush away from them—to the weird-looking contraption of stainless steel which Hood had briefly noted on entering. Tremayne backed in between the two uprights and snapped his wrists and ankles into the clips. He stood there flexing his wrists and working the great metal pincers and he looked straight at Dominat.

"Now, you overgrown conceited clown. Now we're equal."

"Tommy," Hood said jerkily, "what the hell—?"

"Keep out of this, Mark. This is a personal feud."

Lithely and swiftly Dominat moved forward. Still Hood waited. Tremayne must have some private knowledge of that ugly contraption he was handling. And there were four guards behind them. Silent and tensed, Hood watched the beginning of a fantastic duel.

The thing called Titan was beautifully machined and articulated; and Tremayne was a boxer. Every move he made was instantly and faithfully duplicated by the machine. Tremayne had become a giant, more powerful even than his adversary.

And it seemed his adversary, the inventor, was wholly

aware of this. He punched and swayed and feinted but always he kept clear of the dreadful snapping claws. Until, fair and square on the biceps of Dominat's left arm, Tremayne caught him.

There was a brief thin scream of pain. Viciously, Tremayne squeezed harder. Blood oozed. Tremayne laughed. But he was too intent on this single success, and should have captured Dominat's other arm. Swift and hard the bunched fist at the end of this arm slammed down on Tremayne's biceps. Numbed, his muscles relaxed their grip. The claw opened and Dominat jumped clear. His head swiveled.

"No!" he snarled to the guards. "Stay where you are."

He turned back and the weird boxing match continued.

And now all the advantage lay with Dominat. Tremayne was mentally drained and his body was still weak. A huge fist took him in the chest and only Titan's stability prevented him from being hurled over backward. Still Hood waited. He felt absolutely certain that the giant would not kill Tremayne in this fight; he was the type to choose a slower, more pleasurable method.

Hood was right. A fist flashed in against Tremayne's solar plexus. He sagged in the clips. Dominat stepped forward and swiftly tugged Tremayne's wrists and ankles clear. The Englishman sagged to the floor. Dominat bent and lifted him, and turned toward a nearby divan. His arms were full.

And now Hood looked at Murimoto.

A human body is soft. The vital essence of karate is not power, but speed. Take Murimoto. Without shoes, his feet were capable of smashing a wooden plank, either with the ball of the foot or the side of it. As he whirled—even before he started to whirl—his right foot was off the ground. With a vicious *mae geri* it took the second Carib in line in the belly, and ruptured him. Before this man had time to double up in fatal agony Murimoto's other foot was arching up with a left *mae geri* to the abdomen of the third man in line. As he collapsed on his mate the fourth Carib came for Murimoto with a knife.

The blade lunged. It darted in swiftly, but to those cool brown eyes it looked something the same as an acre of moving earth would look to a fly. Murimoto swayed sideways. The knife went past his right shoulder. But he was continuing his sideways arc, right down until his spread fingers met the carpet. As they did, his right foot swept up and crashed against the Carib's throat.

There was no gurgling, no sound at all, for the whole laryngeal apparatus had been crushed. Gaping noiselessly, gasping for breath that could not get through, the Carib joined his mates.

Murimoto's flashing disposal had taken perhaps four seconds. So that Hood, merely a black belt second dan, had just completed his *shuto* chop against the neck of the first man in line as Murimoto bent to tug off his shoes.

Turning back to face the main threat, Hood took in the heap of three bodies with an incredulity he really should not have felt. But there was some excuse for his astonishment, for he had only trained against the master; he had not seen him in purposeful action.

"Jesus," he muttered, then looked for Dominat.

So quick had it been, the colossus was only now straightening up from dumping Tremayne on the divan. Hood saw that Tremayne was all right, struggling up on one elbow, and then he saw the look in Dominat's eyes. He couldn't blame him. The heap of handpicked guards was writhing a little, but plainly finished, while in front of them, composed and apparently unharmed, stood his two victims.

"What happened?" said Dominat.

"Can't you see?" replied Hood.

"You did that?"

"My Japanese friend you despise so much. This is how," said Hood, and slid forward.

"Mark!" Murimoto said sharply.

But Hood was not renowned for circumspection,

especially at a time like this. He could see his friend's beaten body. His blood was up. He had come a long way for this. He went in to finish it.

The force of his rage clouded his caution and faulted his judgment. Hood was a big man but the man waiting for him was a foot taller, and bulkier in proportion. Once they landed against a human body Hood's hands were almost as dangerous as Murimoto's; he should have used them against his enemy's bulk, not against the sneering face.

Normally that right *uraken ganmen uchi*, snapped against an opponent's face, would have been devastatingly effective. But here the face was unnaturally higher, and the judgment of distance behind the blow inexcusably clouded. Hood's fist was taken on Dominat's bunched shoulder, and then gripped in a huge hand, and twisted, and only a quick savage *nukite* with stiff fingers into the abodmen saved Hood's arm from being wrenched out of its socket. He jumped clear.

Murimoto opened his mouth. He shut it. He knew what was troubling his pupil, but interruption would only increase the disadvantage. But Murimoto sidled in closer as Hood, warned, set himself for the *kin geri*, genital foot kick.

Fast and sure Hood's foot flashed out and just as fast Dominat swept his thighs together. Hood's shoe slid up the fleshy incline and its toe thudded into Dominat's lower abdomen. There came a *whoof* of expelled breath but the colossus was unhurt. Viselike his hands gripped around Hood's ankle. He was unskilled in karate but he was enormously strong, and right now strength was all he needed. A quick pace backward had Hood off balance and a heave of the great arms had him off the floor. Dominat whirled, and Hood's spread-eagled body sailed around like the female half of an apache dance team. Then Dominat let go.

Hood had time and sense enough to bunch himself. Even so, though he landed with his bones unbroken, his body shot on until it cannoned against the big main door.

The breath exploded from him. He shook his head and gasped in oxygen. Staring back at Dominat, who had made no move to follow him, Hood reached up to the handle of the door and pulled himself upright.

"Stay there," commanded Murimoto. Hood lurched forward. "Stay!"

In that word there was a tone Hood had never heard Murimoto use before. He halted, his head down like a bull, his mouth open, and his eyes malevolently on the man who had beaten him. Dominat said:

"What, little man? You will take over?"

He spoke to Murimoto. The Japanese said thoughtfully, "You are a very strong man. I do not think I have seen a man so strong."

"And you would try to take me?"

Murimoto nodded gently. "I have to, you see. In the village you caused me to lose much face."

Dominat sneered, then his face hardened. "Come, little yellow man, come on and die."

While Hood and Tremayne watched, Murimoto moved forward until he was two paces in front of Dominat. Even standing up straight his head would barely have reached Dominat's chin. He was in the *kiba dachi*, or riding-horse position, with feet wide apart, knees bent, and both arms held straight down with the fists just above his inclined thighs, his head level with Dominat's lower chest. Sideways and above him the giant loomed so large that Hood thought irrelevantly of David and Goliath.

"A filthy little monkey," Dominat snarled, and with a great sideways hook of his fist, he struck.

It was slaughter.

After the first blow Tremayne was aghast, and even Hood, though he had been commanded to stay, wondered if he should step in and try to stop it. He remained where he was, not sure if that coldly precise killing machine might not turn on him.

For that first blow of Dominat's was the last one he struck. Murimoto's left arm had come up in the *shuto*

soto uke, and rigid as a bar of steel it had blocked the
sweeping blow of the giant. Nor, even under such a
violent impact, did Murimoto's body sway an inch. At
this Hood was not surprised, for he himself, in that low
center of gravity stance, had once withstood a flying
tackle from Tremayne in the gym of the International Club.

Dominat's mouth had opened in astonishment. Now,
abruptly, it grimaced in agony as the hand that could
split a stone caught with its dreadful calloused edge
the left-hand side of his rib cage. Dominat doubled forward with his arms across his crushed chest. Murimoto
stepped half a pace to one side. His hand came up level
with his chin. It paused there, while on his face Hood
saw an expression of such intense concentration that it
approached serenity. Then, swifter than a snake, Murimoto's hand struck. The edge of it, a blunt ax, met the
side of Dominat's upper arm. And that arm dangled,
spurting blood, for the great humerus bone, even pro-
tected by muscle, is softer than a stone, and Dominat's
humerus bone was shattered.

His eyes were clouded with the involuntary tears of
smashing pain. He blundered about the room like a
blinded bull, with his good arm held curved like a crab's
as he sought the man who with deliberate and scientific
precision crashed blow after blow against his great body.
And most of the upper part of this was pulped when
finally Dominat stumbled against the aluminum desk and
hung there, shaking his head to clear his eyes as he
glared with consummate fear at the "filthy little monkey"
sliding toward him.

Dominat's body was broken but his mind was clear,
and the fear of death galvanized it. His fingers found the
console and pressed. A drawer slid out. His hand went
in.

"Look out!" Hood shouted.

Murimoto should have dealt with that remaining good
arm. The hand that could find Tremayne's gun from
twenty paces had no trouble at all in finding Murimoto's
shoulder at three. The shot crashed. It was a big slug,

.45-caliber, and not even the *kiba dachi* stance could have withstood such a forceful impact. Murimoto was flung halfway around. This saved his life, for the next bullet just creased across his chest. Then Hood was there, leaping like a panther, and crashing his palm edge down on the wrist that held the gun; then placing the heel of his hand beneath Dominat's chin and heaving him backward onto the floor. Dominat lay there, moaning feebly with his eyes closed. Hood grabbed Murimoto's arm.

"Let's get the hell out of here!"

Murimoto did not shake his head to clear it, as might have been expected of a man so recently and concentratedly engaged, and then wounded; he looked at Hood composedly, and calmly he answered:

"Yes. Is that door unlocked?"

They found it was. Though the fighting had been quiet, those shots might have been heard, and they ran through the exotic grillwork and into the elevator.

"Which button?" Hood panted, glaring at Tremayne.

"Damned if I know."

"Great!" Hood's finger stabbed the lowest button. The elevator descended with smooth swiftness. "Wish to hell I had my gun!"

No one answered him. Murimoto stood with his feet slightly apart and his face soberly thoughtful as he wadded up his handkerchief and placed it over his wound to stop the flow of blood.

Suddenly the elevator stopped. Automatically the door opened. Cautiously Tremayne peered out. "This isn't the level we came in," he whispered. "We're above it."

"But I pressed the lowest button."

"Then press it again."

Hood did so. Nothing happened. "There must be a separate control to this thing," he said. "They're on to us."

"Then out into the passage," Tremayne snapped, "before we're taken up again."

Hood swung out into the passage. Murimoto came last, and had just cleared the door when it slid shut. A faint whining indicated the elevator's upward progress.

"That's all we need," Hood said grimly. "A man might as well be in Fort Knox."

"Wait a minute." Tremayne was looking along the few yards of brightly lit tunnel. "I think I've been here before. Yes, there's the door."

"Leading where?"

"Come on."

They followed Tremayne because there was nowhere else to go. His hand went to the doorknob and Hood said, "You're in no shape; let me handle it."

Hood turned the knob gently. It moved easily. He edged the door open half an inch, then flung it wide and leaped in, darting to one side as his feet hit the floor. Nothing happened. No one was there.

"Okay," he snapped over his shoulder.

They hurried in and Hood shut the door. He could see no way to lock it. Even if he could it would be pointless; the net result of locking themselves in would be death from starvation or thirst. He looked around the compartment.

"Where are we?"

"That," answered Tremayne, pointing to the black box on its granite pedestal, "is the prototype of Dominat's power plant. It's quite ingenious." He went around to the front of the box, and looked for the switch he remembered having seen Dominat use. "I'll show you how it works."

"Some other time, huh?" said Hood tightly. He looked at Murimoto, who without orders was standing close by one side of the closed door. "No killing, chum," Hood ordered. "Whoever comes in there we want as a hostage." Murimoto nodded. Watching the door, Hood said to Tremayne behind him, "Is there more than one elevator?"

"I doubt it. At least I didn't see one."

"Then they'll have to use ours, and they'll guess we're in here. Now that Dominat's done for, d'you think we have a chance of bluffing his crew?"

"*If* he's done for. He's tough, and he was alive when we left."

"Never mind that. Any chance?"

Tremayne frowned. "Perhaps. I got the impression everyone is scared stiff of him. Could be we might be able to convince them the police know where you are."

At that moment, without warning, the door was flung open.

Possibly for the first time in his life, the master of karate failed. Yet this was understandable, for he had no time. It was Mero. The submachine gun he was holding was framed on Murimoto's chest.

There was silence in the room, broken only by a slight humming which no one heard. Hood's mind was meshing, but fruitlessly. He was too far off to jump the newcomer, and he knew that Murimoto with his wound could do no better.

He took a pace forward, which placed him directly in front of Tremayne. The black barrel did not waver from Murimoto but a pair of pale eyes sent their warning to Hood.

"By the way he's covering Murimoto I'd say he knows *he* fixed Dominat," Tremayne whispered. "Stay just where you are, Mark."

"What?"

"For God's sake, don't argue. Stay there."

Knowing nothing of what Tremayne might have in mind, Hood opened his mouth to give his own desperate orders. Mero interrupted him. The clawlike fingers of one hand jabbed at the three of them, then at Murimoto; and then at the Japanese he spat a stream of hoarsely vehement gibberish. Quite plainly, that unintelligible mouthing said:

"This one first, then you."

And the raised gun barrel shouted the same thing. And as Murimoto's body tensed, and Hood's, and Mero's trigger finger tightened, Tremayne's hand went up swiftly behind him and flicked a switch.

The machine gun yammered, briefly. But the shots went high, ricocheting off the ceiling with short sharp screams; but above those sounds there pierced a shriller scream, an animal-like irruption of agony that lacerated the watchers' nerves.

The screaming stopped. There was no chest anymore to produce sound. There was a horrid sizzling sound, and a smell that would for a long time make these people shudder at the mention of barbecued meat. And as Mero's body sagged downward, the dreadful blade of Dominat's heat box moved upward over his chest and throat and face, until on the floor there was only a scorched mess, and Tremayne flicked off the switch. The panel dropped shut.

Hood, even Murimoto, turned their heads away, trying not to breathe. But Tremayne stood looking at what he had done. Icy and controlled, remembering the degradation he had experienced, first with Borja, then with Dominat, he said, very softly:

"I had to do it. Besides, I was beginning to feel rather inadequate."

"Take the gun," Hood said to Temayne. "You know how that funicular thing works?"

"Yes."

They stepped out into the passage and there they saw Dominat again.

He was still alive. Only just. Maddened and blinded with pain, he was rushing along the passage, stumbling into the walls as he came toward them.

Through some instinct, or hearing the sounds of their voices, Dominat halted in his headlong rush. He was shaking his head and clawing at his eyes as if he thought he could rip away his blindness. Then he screamed.

It was a scream of terror. Hood had never heard anything like it. It made him feel cold all over. It was the scream of the damned.

Suddenly, Dominat wheeled and blundered back along the passage away from them.

"Come on," Hood urged the others, running along the passage after him.

At the end of the passage, where it opened out into an upper level of the Swiss-cheese cavern into which Dominat had led Tremayne earlier that day and showed him the atoborer at work, there was an iron platform and a narrow iron staircase that ran down to the floor.

Still screaming, babbling with terror, the huge man swung himself down the staircase. Hood and the others halted at the platform and gazed down at Dominat's reeling figure.

As he lurched toward them, the workers in the cavern backed away in fright.

"Hell, what's he going to do?"

"He's making for the atoborer," Tremayne observed.

"What's that?"

"I'll tell you later."

The noise began as a low subdued hum. Tremayne clapped his hands over his ears and backed into the passage. "Come back," he yelled at the top of his voice to the others. "For God's sake."

The noise increased. They could feel the vibrations thudding into their bones. Pushing Murimoto ahead of him, Hood backed away from the platform.

The last thing he saw before Tremayne grabbed his arm and hauled him inside was that Dominat had grabbed the machine, the atoborer, and in one last superhuman effort, was aiming it at the wall. Then he stumbled and the machine dug into the floor. In two seconds it had disappeared, with Dominat's body, vibrating so violently that it was only an indistinct blur, still hanging onto it.

"Come on," Tremayne yelled again. "We've got to get out of here."

Hood, Tremayne, and Murimoto were back on board the treacherous Mona's cruiser, the *Goosewing*, heading out to sea. More than half an hour had elapsed. They had escaped from the mountain and, surprisingly enough, had encountered no resistance as they ran through the village—most of the inhabitants seemed to be having their evening meal. The dinghy was still at the pier and Hood took them out to the lolling craft.

Just as they were climbing aboard, they could hear a deep-throated rumbling from the mountain and see the earth under the village move slightly, causing the huts to shiver. At once people ran out and turned to look at the mountain; there was much waving of arms and shouting, and then they poured down to the beach and into the fishing boats drawn up on the sand. The mountain continued to rumble, then, as jagged streaks of light flashed across the sky above it, the sound swelled to a roar. There was a bright white flash and a hissing noise. The shock waves from the exploding mountain swiped at the fishing boats, almost swamping them, and at the cruiser, sending it skidding sideways across the water. The three Intertrust men were sent sprawling.

"What happened?" Hood yelped.

Where the top of the mountain had been was a great red and yellow ball of fire; most of the mountain itself had been swallowed up in its own crater.

Tremayne told him, "I could see it coming. As soon as Dominat fell with that atoborer. You know about Krakatoa. It seems there's always a fire deep down in a volcano's root. In Krakatoa's case the sea managed to get in through a fissure it had ruptured open with its weight—in fact, the sea had been trying to do this for a long time. Anyway, you can imagine what happened when it did—water turned to steam, more water, more steam, until enough pressure had built up to rip the island in two. Now, the atoborer must have gone straight down until it met the root of the crater. Then, with the sea pressure down there being what it was—well, it was inevitable."

"What a bang," was Hood's comment.

"Well, it certainly solved our problems for us." Tremayne began to explain everything that had happened to him from the time he had been kidnapped by Borja. He gave a sketchy account of Dominat's professed aims, and shook his head. "All those fantastic gadgets—blown sky-high."

Hood shrugged. " 'The moving finger writes and having writ, moves on.' That," he explained to Murimoto, "was also penned by Omar Khayyám."

Later, as he stood out on the deck, staring far out into the starry glory of the night, in his own way, silently and privately, Mark Hood gave thanks.